CROW JANE

ROCK BAND FIGHTS EVIL #3

CROW JANE

ROCK BAND FIGHTS EVIL #3

D.J. Butler

WordFire Press
Colorado Springs, Colorado

CROW JANE
Copyright © 2012 D.J. Butler

ISBN: 978-1-61475-299-8

Cover painting by Carter Reid

Cover design by Janet McDonald

Art Director Kevin J. Anderson

Book Design by RuneWright, LLC
www.RuneWright.com

Published by
WordFire Press, an imprint of
WordFire, Inc.
PO Box 1840
Monument CO 80132

Kevin J. Anderson & Rebecca Moesta, Publishers

WordFire Press Trade Paperback Edition April 2015
Printed in the USA
wordfirepress.com

CHAPTER ONE

Jane looked with eyes that had seen many things. She had watched the Holy League sink the Turk at Lepanto. She had seen Spartacus and his six thousand revolutionaries nailed to crosses on the Appian Way. She had witnessed the falls of Troy, Ugarit, Ebla, and Babel, when she had still been recognized by the children of men, and known by the name her mother had given her. It had been a long, long time since anything had truly delighted Jane's eyes.

This rock and roll band certainly didn't. They tried to make up in enthusiasm what they lacked in finesse, but their efforts left her unsatisfied. Time was infinite, mankind was a huge, flowing river, and Jane had heard it all before. Still, she had followed them all the way from New Mexico, and this was her first actual glance at them, so she paid close attention.

"Ten thousand miles of motorway tar," the singer roared.
Maori girl and a Japanese car,
Picking a living on this old guitar,
I gotta go.
I gotta go."

He was tall and lean, with the broad-shouldered, muscular physique of a rugby player or a Myrmidon. He looked the part of a rock and roller, pale and intense, with eyes like ice and black hair to his shoulders. There was something familiar about him too, something Jane could not quite place. His wide mouth nearly swallowed the microphone, and his booming voice threatened to shake the brick walls of the bar.

"I loved you well but from afar,
Picadilly or Zanzibar?
I gotta go."

The crow flapped directly over the players on the tiny stage, mocking her with its enormous black wings. She couldn't avoid seeing it, but she resolutely avoided paying it any conscious attention.

"Enjoyin' the music?" a voice asked at her elbow.

Jane turned and saw that it had come from the man behind the bar. "Layers of sound piled on top of each other do not necessarily become music," she told him, "just as a series of events is not necessarily a story."

"You don't follow the band, then?"

"I don't."

"Too bad," he said, "I'se hopin' maybe you could tell me their names. I coulda swore when we booked them yesterday they were The Racket Club, but tonight they're callin' themselves Laughing Jack and the Sons of Bitches."

"Maybe they're on the lam."

The bartender chuckled deferentially. "If they are, I reckon they're not the only ones in the room. That's quite the set of tattoos you're sportin'," he said.

Jane looked at him more closely. She didn't particularly care for the bartender, and it had been centuries since she'd had a conversation with a human being that was anything other than dry dust and hollow words, but she wanted a distraction from the crow. Also, the fact that he had noticed her at all caused a tiny spark of surprise to flash in her mind—he must be a keen observer, and she must have let herself drift too close. "And you have quite an accent, barkeep. You're not from here."

"I ain't from Kansas," the bartender agreed. He was a tallish man with a shock of silver hair and a twinkle in his eye. He wore jeans and a checked shirt, and Jane could see in the *Wild Turkey*-branded mirror behind him that he stood within easy reach of a sawed-off, double-barreled shotgun under the bar. "I wandered the hills of

North Carolina in my youth, and I reckon in my old age I jest started wanderin' a bit further. Name's John," he grinned. "What're you drinkin'?"

Jane was already bored. No amount of wandering could compete with hers. She looked back at the stage again and saw the crow perched on the guitar player's amplifier. He was a wiry thin black man in torn blue jeans and a green military jacket, bristling with pocket flaps, the sleeves of which had been crudely ripped off. He played a worn red guitar and stared down at it with intense focus. Behind him lurked the bass player, a tall, slightly paunchy man with thick black hair. If any of the band was a real musician it was him—he threw improvised little flourishes into the turnarounds like he too was bored with the song, and was trying to liven it up—but he looked shaky, and barely under control. Drugs, Jane thought, or some deep-seated fear.

The burning sands of the hippodrome,
Slick my hair back, polish my chrome,
One final battle, one final poem,
I gotta go.
I gotta go.

"Call me Jane," she said. "And pour me rum."

"Got a bit of an accent yourself, don't you?" John asked, pouring black liquid out of a bottle with sea monsters inked on the label.

"I was young in another time and place," she said. "I only learned English as an adult." When she was a child, no human foot had yet trod upon the forested knob of land that would one day become England.

"I wouldn't want you to feel I'se pryin', but I'm guessin' the South Pacific … am I right?" John asked.

Jane threw back the rum. She'd learned to like the drink while sailing Spanish treasure galleons, centuries ago now. It seemed like yesterday to her, but a yesterday from which she was separated by a yawning gulf of infinite tedium.

"I mean, from the tattoos. Ain't a lot of people get tattoos like those, are there? Big swirlin' patterns on the face and all? That's distinctive."

"They were put on me as a mark," Jane said, the word *mark* bitter in her mouth. "They were meant to be distinctive."

"Plus your complexion's that nice caramel color," John said. "I don't mean nothin' rude by it—chalk it up to my age if you're offended, or the hits to the head I took in Nam—and I think you're pretty. I'm jest sayin' you look Polynesian. Or Latina, maybe, or some kind of mix. Am I right?"

I know I told you I was born to roam,
But now I'm burning to get back home.
I gotta go.

At the back of the stage with the bass player were the electric organ and the drums. The organ player was a boxy little mesomorph with brown hair, a thin black tie and a neat blue suit, tight at the wrists and ankles. He was nearly invisible under piles of electronic devices and cable and his sound was huge, but patchy.

The drummer, by contrast, sat at a very spare drum kit and played with two wooden sticks that looked like fighting clubs. She wore spiked leather from head to toe and had the androgynous facial features and animal tail that marked her as one of Mab's folk. That, Jane thought, was almost interesting. What was one of the fey doing playing in a crummy rock and roll band in Dodge City, Kansas? The Legate hadn't said anything about that, and it made her take a second look at the other members of the band. What were *they* hiding?

"Men have always found me pretty," Jane agreed. "That's the root of the problem."

The song ended in a predictable clash of cymbals and some modest scattered applause. The guitar player shuffled over to the singer and took the microphone. Jane noticed their footgear—the singer's looked like what a horseman might wear to ride, and the guitar player had combat boots.

"We'll take a break now," the guitarist announced, "but we'll be back on the stage in a few minutes."

"Another?" John asked cheerfully.

"I've had enough," Jane said. She slapped a bill onto the bar and stepped away into the crowd, her spurs jingling slightly.

Her wards of dissembling made her hard to notice, and she let the sweaty, alcohol-breathed herd swallow her. Wellman's wasn't full, but it was full enough to give her space in which to be inconspicuous, despite the ankle-length black duster she wore and the black broad-brimmed hat, the knives strapped to her belt and boots and forearms and the swirling tattoos that covered her entire face as they covered her entire body. She had given up cursing those angels who had held her down and marked her millennia ago, but only because her curses were pointless. If she ever saw one of them, she'd kill him.

That was why she'd come to Kansas.

Not that her knives would work on an angel. Of course, the knives weren't her only weapons. Deliberately, she brushed the pistol holstered on her hip, the Horn. And that was why the Legate had come looking for her.

That, and the fact that he had something to offer her that she couldn't refuse.

The crow flapped slowly in circles in the high space above the bar. The drinkers, primarily college kids but including a few self-consciously hip-looking older people, went about their business and mostly ignored the band that stepped off the stage into their midst. The big handsome singer got offered a few beers and took one, nodding and smiling as three college girls asked for the blessing of his presence, but saying nothing. Was he shy? The others were left to their own devices. Three of them headed for the bar, the heavy bass player in the lead and walking fast.

The fairy moved off alone.

Wellman's had been built in a structure that had once housed a railroad station. Its walls were two stories tall and made of brick, and its windows and ceiling had a Gothic look about their arched apices. Bare light bulbs hung in straight rows from very long wires, and the crow wheeled slowly around them. A length of track still ran along one wall in a bed of gravel, terminating at either end in blank brick. The restrooms squatted off a short hall tunneling out perpendicularly from the bar, over a bridge of planks that had been nailed into place to limit the tripping opportunities for drunk patrons with urgently pressing bladders.

The fairy skipped over the bridge and headed into the restrooms.

Jane followed. She prepared as she went, slipping an iron knife—not steel, *iron*—into her right hand and a digging a small glass vial from the pocket of her duster with her left. She checked the vial visually as she passed under a light bulb to be sure she'd grabbed the right one—the glob of quicksilver inside slid back and forth and she smiled without pleasure.

The wards of dissembling were her general travel disguise because they were so simple to erect and so costless to maintain and they did the job—mostly Jane didn't bother people. She just didn't want to be noticed. Unfortunately, the wards of dissembling would lose effectiveness if she walked directly up to the fairy. As the drummer stepped into the mouth of the restroom's hall, she cast a long, pale shadow by the hallway's lights. Jane stepped firmly onto the shadow and spoke a few words.

If anyone in the hall had heard the words, they would have been unable to decipher them, or even remember the sounds, two seconds later. She had spoken in the tongue of her birth, a language that hadn't been spoken on earth for millennia, and which most humans were no longer able, by divine fiat, to understand. The language was Adamic, and Jane understood it because she had been born before the Great Tower, the Confusion of the Tongues, and the First Scattering. She was subject to the Fall of Adam—indeed, she was its firstfruits—but not to the Curse of Babel.

She spoke her spells in Adamic because it was one of the Primals, and a powerful language for magic. As soon as she had spoken this one, and willed some of the force of her *ka* into it, some of the fire and energy that was the power-component of the collection of spiritual things most mortals knew as their *soul*, she became invisible. Everything looked the same to her, but she knew that to any other observer who had been able to see her at that moment, she would have vanished into the fairy's shadow.

The shadow pulled her now and she walked faster, padding behind the long silver hair and silver horse's tail of the drummer. The fairy pushed at the *GENTLEMEN* door first, found it shut, and then opened *LADIES*. Jane followed her in, nimbly slipping through before the door thudded shut.

The fairy latched the door and Jane drifted out of the way, tightening her grip on her weapons. She wanted the creature fully distracted when she made her move, and she could afford to wait.

Then the drummer turned to the mirror over the sink, looked into it with a fierce eye and spat on the glass. That move piqued

Jane's curiosity, and as the fairy filled her hands with blue-foaming soap from the dispenser over the sink and then smeared it all across the mirror, she considered. Was the fairy an outcast? A criminal? An exile?

What was she doing here? Jane wondered.

And could she still enter the Mirror Queendom?

She had been waiting for the fairy to be distracted, she realized, and instead she had distracted herself. Jane whispered several more words of Adamic and willed into place wards of silence. As the silver-haired drummer shook foam from her hands, splattering it on the broken red tile of the floor, Jane attacked.

She struck with the iron knife first. She didn't stab, because she wanted the fairy alive, at least for the moment. Instead, she leaned forward with her elbows and forearm, leading with the blunt edge of the blade. The first notice that the fairy had of the attack was Jane's iron knife suddenly pressing into the back of her neck.

The iron burned her at the touch. Smoke and a burning smell—not the bitter stink of burning flesh, but a woody odor, like that of a tree on fire—filled Jane's nostrils.

"Aaaaaaaaagh!" the fairy howled. Jane heard her perfectly well, but she knew that as long as she kept physical contact with the creature, no one else would be able to hear her. The fairy jerked and twisted, but the pain sapped all the bite out of her resistance. Jane fell forward with the creature, slamming her face into the soapy mirror and then pinning her to the sink.

"Who are you?" the drummer shrieked, kicking back wildly. Jane cracked her forehead against the white porcelain of the sink and then spun her around, keeping the blade pressed to her white flesh.

"I'm the Marked Woman," Jane growled. "Don't your people teach their cubs and kits about me anymore?"

She said it to instill fear, and because it couldn't hurt her that the fairy knew. Then she slammed her other hand against the drummer's exposed clavicle, shattering the glass of the vial and grinding the quicksilver into the fairy's pale skin.

Wings sprouted from the side of the fairy's head like ears, flapped once and disappeared. A horse's legs exploded out of the leather-bar-style clothing the drummer worse, and then her face became a horse's long, bony phiz, and then a falcon's. She exploded into a shrieking, flailing, formless and many-formed abundance of shapes. She kicked and writhed and twisted but she didn't escape, because Jane didn't let her.

All the while, Jane pressed down with the iron knife and smelled smoke.

And all the while, the elusive, ever-present crow of her death perched on top of the paper-towel dispenser and stared down at her with a sour yellow eye.

Then the animal forms were gone, and the man and woman shapes, too, and Jane held the fairy against the sink in her true form.

She was a female, two feet high, with leathery gray skin and eyes that were completely yellow. Her belly and her dugs sagged, her cat-like ears and whiskers trembled. The one remnant of her more beautiful self, her silver horse's tail, flapped soggily in the running water of the sink.

"What shall I call you?" Jane pulled the knife away, keeping it still in her hand and visible, but she held the quicksilver pressed to the fairy's flesh. It would keep her from changing shape, or attempting to use her Glamour.

"I'm a fairy," she croaked back. "I don't have a true name, sorceress."

Jane stared coldly down at the creature and flared her nostrils. "Don't repeat the mistake of thinking I'm stupid, child of Mab," she said. "I will happily release you from your exile with my iron blade."

The fairy hissed through gapped yellow teeth. "How...?" she wrinkled her nose, looked at her own handiwork on the mirror, and slumped in defeat. "Twitch," she said. "Call me Twitch."

"Very good, Twitch," Jane gave her prisoner positive reinforcement. "Now listen to me closely. I'm going to ask questions. You're going to be tempted to evade them, or to lie. The first time you choose not to answer fully and honestly, I'll cut you." She held the iron knife in front of the fairy's eyes as a reminder. "The second time you do so, I'll kill you. Do you understand?"

The fairy nodded.

"Use words, Twitch." Jane smiled.

"I understand," the drummer agreed.

"Several days ago," Jane began, "something was stolen in New Mexico. Something that Heaven considers very valuable, that had been in its keeping and hidden for thousands of years. The keeper fled." No point identifying the keeper as the angel Raphael, or Jane's real errand, or the bitterness of her feelings. "The thieves escaped. I have tracked them here." No point explaining about the Mare, either. "Are you following me so far, Twitch?"

"Yes," Twitch nodded.

"Now," Jane said slowly. "I'm going to ask you the question that you are going to try to lie about. Remember this, child of Mab. The first time, I'll only cut you."

Twitch gulped.

"Where is the hoof, fairy?" Jane asked.

Twitch hesitated. "I … I don't know," she ventured in her bullfrog voice.

Jane nodded, affecting a sad face, and stabbed the drummer in her arm.

"Aaaaaaaagh!" Twitch shrieked again, a horrendous, piteous cry. She thrashed and wiggled on the sink, but Jane held her pinned, and kept the quicksilver firmly pressed to her chest.

Smoke billowed from the wound rather than blood, and stung Jane's eyes.

"Stop! Please, stop!"

Jane pulled the knife back and regarded the fairy with stern eyes.

"I told you," she reminded the ugly creature, "the first time I would cut you. Do you remember what I'm going to do the second time you choose not to answer me?"

The fairy's eyes rolled desperately in her head. "Kill me," she hissed through chapped and shuddering lips.

"Kill you," Jane agreed. She turned the knife so that its sharp edge now faced the fairy, and gently touched the blade to her neck. She heard a *sizzle* and smelled faint burning. "Now, are you ready to try again?"

Twitch said nothing, only shivered. The crow stared down impassively. After thousands of years and thousands of failed attempts, Jane still had to suppress the urge to throw the knife at the crow instead, to make a heroic lunge and grab the bird with its terrible, joyous burden, tearing into its flesh and feathers with her teeth and devouring it whole, drawing it into her body's permanent embrace.

She blinked and exhaled, driving away the thought.

"I know that you and your friends stole Azazel's hoof from the well in Dudael," Jane said. "Understand me clearly: I *know* it was you. Unless you are content to die here and now, Twitch, child of Mab, tell me where the hoof is."

Twitch swallowed hard and stared into Jane's eyes. "Jim has it," she said.

Good. Once the stone started rolling down the mountain, the fairy would be hard pressed to stop it. "Which one is Jim?"

"The singer," Twitch said, and closed her eyes pathetically.

"Where does he keep it?" Jane asked.

"On his body," the fairy admitted. "He keeps it taped ... taped to his belly."

Jane nodded. She wouldn't have let it away from her person, either. "Is that where the hoof is now?" she asked.

Twitch hesitated, but only for a second. "He hasn't let go of it since we got it," she said. "It's his."

"What do you mean, it's *his?*" Jane asked. "Is he your leader?"

"Yes," Twitch said instantly. "The hoof belongs to his family. Really, his father." Now that she had started talking, she couldn't stop. "Jim is Azazel's son."

This thoroughly mediocre dive-bar band was quickly becoming the most interesting thing Jane had seen in a century. "What are you doing with the hoof?" she asked. She rationalized the question easily: she needed to gauge how much resistance would be put up when she took it, and whether Jim would try to take it back and thereby interfere with her plans. Really, though, she was curious.

"We're going to Chicago," Twitch said. Tears leaked from her yellow eyes and streamed onto the bathroom porcelain. "Eddie knows a hoodoo woman there, and we're going to contact the Infernal powers and make a deal."

"Eddie?"

"The guitar player. He sold his soul and he wants it back."

"And what does Jim want?"

Twitch sobbed openly now. "He wants to be ... he wants peace, I think."

"And you want back?" Jane nodded at the foam-covered mirror. It felt strange to indulge pure curiosity. Strange and sort of pleasant. "Somehow, you can strike a bargain with Azazel that will let you back into the Shadowless Palace."

Twitch nodded and shuddered. "I need his forgiveness," she wept.

That was a queer thing to say and prompted more questions, but Jane shook herself mentally; enough games. Time to take quick action. "Do you know who I am?" she prompted the creature.

"You're the Marked Woman," Twitch nodded. "You're Qayna, the one the humans call *Cain*."

Jane raised the iron knife to plunge it into the fairy's body.

Bam! Bam! Bam! came a hammering at the boor.

"Twitch?" called a man's voice.

CHAPTER TWO

T witch, we're on in three. You in there?"

Jane hesitated a split second, considering whether she should hold the fairy drummer hostage and demand the hoof of Azazel in exchange. In that split second, she realized that the voice at the door didn't belong to Jim the singer, and remembered that he had sat down, grinning, to drink a beer with the table of co-eds, so the person knocking must be someone else in the band.

In that same split second, Twitch bit her.

Jane cursed in Adamic (her native tongue had few true curse words, but they were very strong—Jane's curse splashed cold water around the room as if she had punched her fist into the sink) and pulled back her hand. It was the hand with the bead of quicksilver cupped in it, and the fairy had craned her neck at an impossible angle to sink her yellow teeth into the flesh of Jane's wrist.

She only pulled the hand away half an inch, but that half inch was enough.

A silvery falcon exploded into being beneath Jane's hand, a broad-winged, beautiful bird that was instantly recognizable as a fey creature, and as Twitch, by its possession of the same long silver horse's tail. With a powerful flap of its wings, the falcon snapped out of Jane's hands and up to the top of the paper towel dispenser. It shrieked, a sharp and piercing cry, and then Twitch was again a lithe, androgynous drummer wearing leather and spikes. The crow gazed dully at them both, unfazed that it had to share its perch so long as it wasn't sharing with Jane. And the fairy, of course, didn't see the crow at all.

Twitch struck the wall with her heels and kicked off. Her drumsticks leaped into her hands in mid-air as she soared over Jane's head, striking with a drum major's *rat-tat-tat* of hard blows.

"Twitch? What's going on, *chingón?*" the voice at the door insisted.

Jane blocked several blows of the fairy's batons with her forearm, ducking as the other woman sailed over her. She had an instant's regret that she had let herself be distracted, but then decided that this was a development she could use.

"Mike!" the fairy shouted, landing lightly on her feet by the cracked toilet. "Help!"

She was outside the wards of silence, and Mike heard her. "*Huevos!*" Jane heard him shout, and then a shoulder was thrown against the door.

Jane let the wards of silence drop and kept fighting.

She gained space for herself with a series of sharp thrusts. The fairy parried and retreated until she was forced to hop up and stand on the toilet seat itself, back against the old lead plumbing. Then Jane whirled, throwing her duster up behind her like a cloak to impede and distract her fey combatant. With a swipe of her forearm, she cleared the mirror of foam and then finished her spin arms first, catching and deflecting another flurry of blows from the fairy. She kept her right fist closed around the lump of quicksilver, and the iron blade in her left.

The crow watched, unmoved.

"Hold on!" Mike shouted. "Eddie! It's Twitch!"

Reinforcements were arriving. That suited Jane just fine, so long as they didn't include Jim.

Bang! Bang! Bang!

The doorknob burst inward and clanked to the floor, and then the latch flew off its screws.

Jane forced the fairy back again with the cold bite of her iron knife, muttering an Adamic incantation as she did—

then turned and leaped for the mirror.

The bass player shouldered into the room, leading with his pistol and following with his burly frame. Behind him came the guitarist, shorter and wiry and also holding a gun.

"Are you leaving so soon?" Twitch shouted, and Jane felt the creature strike her in the back, wrapping long fingers around Jane's shoulders as the surface of the mirror faded, became translucent and then transparent, revealing behind it an endless maze of stairs and corridors and two surprised faces—

"Dammit!" someone yelled behind her in the restroom—

and then Jane felt the cool veil of the mirror's unsubstantiated presence pass over her like a film of water and she was through.

But she had come with a passenger.

The fairy bit her again, in the neck.

Jane hit the ground rolling forward, onto her fingertips and the top of her head and then she slammed down onto her back on the stone floor, hard—

smashing Twitch.

"Oomph!" the fairy grunted.

"Halt!"

Two girl-boyish fey faces loomed over her—the faces of Queen's Rangers, no doubt—over spears pointing down. One had flame-orange hair and a fox's tail and the other was striped, head and tail, like a badger; both wore leather jerkins and greaves, the breastplates carved and painted with Mab's emblem, the tree and lightning bolt. Their spears were entirely wooden, their tips sharpened by fire.

The Queen's Rangers were scouts, warriors and sentinels; they patrolled the infinite maze that was the Outer Bounds of the Mirror Queendom.

Jane ignored the Rangers and stood; Twitch was too stunned by the impact with the floor to stop her. The Outer Bounds stretched around her in all directions, an explosion of halls, staircases, shafts and pits with glass windows in every flat surface. This was a defense mechanism, Jane knew, a classic maze to disorient and deter outsiders. Any ordinary human who managed to stumble in through a gate would find himself bewildered and lost, and the fairies could easily kill him or, if it so struck their puckish senses of humor, let him wander forever.

Jane was no ordinary human, and she knew how to make her way.

"I say again, halt!" cried Foxtail in a shrill voice that whistled through his nose. "Friend or foe, and state your business!"

"My business is my own," Jane said coolly. She sheathed her iron knife, but slowly, making sure that the fairies saw it first.

It had the intended effect; they both shuffled back a step and tightened their grip on their spears.

Jane kept the quicksilver in her fist—she'd need it to get through the Bounds, anyway—and deliberately doffed her broad-brimmed hat, letting her long black hair fall out behind her in its loose plait and allowing the Rangers get a good look at the tattoos all over her face. "And I'm no one's friend. I'm a fugitive and a vagabond … hadn't you heard?"

Both Rangers gasped. "The Marked Woman," Badger growled uneasily.

"Let me pass," Jane told them, replacing her hat. "You have no choice, anyway. You can't kill me, and if you get in my way I'll surely kill you. This one, though," she turned and kicked Twitch hard in the belly, "this one is one of yours."

She straightened her duster and walked on. She knew that she had the initiative, but she would only retain it if she kept moving.

"How did you even get in here, Outcast?" she heard Badger grunt behind her, and then came pummeling sounds that boded ill for Twitch.

Light shone in through all the windows around Jane. Each window let in luminescence of a different quality—noon's blaze here, starlight there, and in a third place a fluorescent flutter—resulting in a dim and shifting patchwork of illumination in the maze Jane now traversed. Nowhere was there darkness, but nowhere was there any light a traveler could trust. She whispered instructions in her birth tongue to the drop of quicksilver, infused it with her ka, and then followed its directions as it strained within her hand.

The fey were overwhelmingly convinced of their own cleverness, but a little insight and a few basic tools were all one needed to handle them.

Before she'd activated the quicksilver, the crow had sat on a high step and stared at her. Now it preceded Jane up a staircase, across a needle-thin bridge, under a series of arches so low Jane had to stoop, across a vault the size of a football stadium and into a warren of twisting halls only a cubit wide. At her every step she heard the muffled swishing of things moving, just out of her sight, not quite in sync with the metallic jingle of her spurs; Jane ignored the sounds. The crow stopped at the window she was looking for, the gate she had willed her quicksilver guide to locate.

With a single word, Jane cleared the frosted surface of the window and looked through. She saw what she expected and hoped to see: the silvered back of the bartender John's head, a row of bleary-eyed college boys flipping cups at the bar, and beyond them, a table with a circle of giggling young women chattering at the tall singer, Jim.

Azazel's son. Azazel had had another son.

And Jim had the hoof.

Jane didn't have an empty vial. She drew the FN Model 1910, the Calamity Horn, the weapon Heaven had loathed and now coveted, and fired off a round into the maze. *Bang!* the discharge echoed loud, but there was no mortal in earshot to be driven mad by it. The sound that Jane was looking for was the tinny rattle of the brass shell as it hit the floor. The noise might discombobulate Foxtail and Badger, but she was indifferent to their concerns.

Jane holstered the gun. She stooped, picked up the shell, and poured the quicksilver bead into it. She tamped a bit of wax from a candle stub in her pocket into the top to seal it; that would have to do for now. She pocketed candle and shell again and turned to face the window. She stretched to look down at the floor at John's feet, watching his movement and his shadow. When he stood to calmly refuse another beer to a buzzcut boy who looked like he was on the verge of throwing up his last one, she cast the opening spell—

stepped through the gate, still mumbling in Adamic—

and touched down in John the barkeep's shadow, safely invisible.

John stiffened, straightening his back and looking around him. The Appalachian wanderer knew too much; Jane stepped quickly away from him, exiting the print of his shadow and slipping out of his arm's reach, letting the wards of dissembling take over again. She crouched quickly, stepping under the hinged flap in the bar leading out onto the floor at walking speed.

She looked back from the other side. For just a moment, she thought the bartender was looking directly at her.

Jane frowned, but then John's eye wandered away, and the crow flew out through the mirror and soared above the tables.

She looked to her right, at the restroom hallway. The guitarist came hustling out of the ladies' room with the bass player on his trail. They were headed directly for Jane, not seeing her for her wards of dissembling.

"Hey!" the heavy bass player called. That was *Mike*, then, the one who cursed in Spanish and looked like a drunk.

"Don't be such a damned coward!" the black man hissed back. "What do you think's going to happen if you're alone for a minute?"

"You have no idea, Eddie!" Mike shook his head. The guitar player was *Eddie*.

Eddie grabbed the short organ player at the corner of the bar. He was dressed like an extra on an eighties television show, but he drank like a yogin—the glass in front of him had an egg in it, as well as fibers that might be some kind of grass, and it smelled like vinegar. "Adrian!" Eddie snapped. "In the can, pronto! It's Twitch!"

"A friend in need," Adrian chuckled, "and so forth. Especially Twitch." He gulped his egg mess in one swallow, pulled his sleeves down to his wrists, and turned to follow his friends.

"Jim!" Eddie yelled, waving across the bar at the singer as they went.

Then Adrian stopped. Jane had a sense of foreboding and stepped into the edge of a booth full of men in cheap suits chattering over mozzarella sticks and olives. She hid her body behind the wooden column that formed the corner of the booth and peered around it.

Adrian pulled something from his pocket and held it up to his eye. As it touched his face, Jane saw it glint and realize that it was a piece of glass, a lens of some sort. She ducked back further into the booth, chanting quickly in Adamic to throw up the deepest, strongest wards of obfuscation and seeming she could. Her ka raged indignantly within her at the suddenness with which she tapped its strength, and she ignored it. Its fury felt like bad indigestion or a heart attack, but she knew it couldn't kill her.

Then she held her breath.

Long seconds passed in which nothing happened, except that her omnipresent crow dropped onto the high seat of an adjacent booth and stared at her.

Soon enough, she thought, but she kept her mouth shut.

When she looked back around the column behind which she was hiding, she saw the organ player—the *wizard*—Adrian, moving with Eddie and Mike towards the restroom, and concluded he must not have seen her. They were going to rescue Twitch; Eddie and Mike needed their spellcaster Adrian to open the gate into the Outer Bounds. Jane was still acting, the rock and rollers reacting.

She relaxed a touch and released her wards.

"Holy shit!" the man nearest her spat out. He had big hands, a brush-like brown mustache and a slumping cigarette clamped between his teeth. "What just happened to me? Did I black out?"

"What happened to *you?*" asked his friend, a burly man with tomato stains on his blue shirt. "Jeez, I think I had an aneurysm! You all disappeared!"

A third man pulled a plastic cylinder from his pocket and tapped several white pills into his hand.

Jane almost laughed out loud at their collective confusion. In her haste, she realized, she had thrown wards over the entire table, and the men sitting at it had been blinded for the duration.

Not her problem. She saw Jim crossing the floor towards the restroom, a flock of young women around him, and she moved to intercept. He didn't look fey, nor Angelic, so she drew two long knives, muttered up a quick ward of seeming to make herself look innocuous, a drunk and stumbling fraternity buffoon, in a stained baggy t-shirt and expensive jeans.

"I get it, I get it!" one of the girls giggled. Her jacket was a shell of sequins around a bubbling core of young fluff. "This is like Calvin Coolidge, right? Isn't there some story about Coolidge not talking much?"

Jim arched an eyebrow and nodded in the direction of the restrooms. Jane didn't relish the idea of stabbing Azazel's son; nor did she relish the thought of another six thousand years of lonely wandering.

"Silent Cal," her friend agreed. She had big hair that looked like it would coordinate well with the suit and tie of the wizard Adrian. Fashion, like everything else, was a boring, unstoppable cycle.

"And at this party, right? This woman comes up to President Coolidge and says 'I bet my friend I can get you to say more than two words.'" She seemed proud of herself for remembering this banal story about a dead, unimportant president.

Jane remembered Calvin Coolidge; the best she could say about him was that he didn't have delusions of grandeur. Which, on reflection, was an unusual quality in a politician.

Jim smiled politely and kept walking towards the hallway. He clenched and unclenched his fists, which Jane read as a sign that he was itching for action and wished he had a weapon in his hand. She was happier, of course, that he didn't.

She stumbled onto the tracks a few feet away, feigning drunkenness, as Jim reached the railroad tracks and the little plank bridge. She saw clearly now that he had something under his shirt, against his belly.

"What was Coolidge's answer?" Big Hair looked like she was on the edge of her seat.

"'You lose,'" Jane said, and she stabbed Jim with both knives.

She'd heard the story, too.

Jane's knives were not enchanted, but they were good sharp steel and they cut flesh effortlessly. Jim yelped and fell back, and Jane grabbed for his belly—

but Jim wasn't *collapsing*, he was *rolling*, and as Jane's fingers brushed fibrous, sticky bands on the hard, flat stomach of the barband singer, he was gone, out of reach. Her two knives went with him, one in his hip and one in his side, and she narrowly avoiding getting kicked in the face.

Hot red blood spilled onto the planks, unhidden by Jane's wards.

Big Hair shrieked first, but Sequins screamed louder.

Jane rushed forward to close the gap, whipping smaller knives from their sheaths on her forearms and slashing overhand, trying to cut the big man. He moved like an acrobat, though, staying just beyond the glittering razor edge of her blades. His first tumble backward landed him in a handstand, one hand on each of the metal rails of the abandoned train track that ran across the floor of the bar, and then he sprang further away again, landed on the tips of his boots, and shuffled backward immediately. The spurting arc of blood trailing behind him spattered across Jane's duster and, from the suddenly ramping volume of the shrieking behind her, might also have ruined the girls' outfits.

Slash, slash, duck and dodge, and then suddenly Jim snatched two beer bottles off a table as he passed and hurled them at her. Jane batted one aside with an elbow and let the other hit her in the shoulder. The crow swooped between her and her target in a cruel and taunting maneuver, obscuring her aim for a moment and pricking her in one of the few remaining sensitive spots in her soul.

In the fraction of an instant during which she hesitated, Jim pulled the knives from his own body and charged to attack.

The yelling was more general now, and Jane could hear the voice of the bartender in the tumult. "Everybody cool it!" he barked in his Appalachian twang. "Now!"

Boom!

That would be one barrel of the man's shotgun. Jane wasn't at all worried about the firearm, nor was she too concerned about the bartender himself, despite his unusual perceptiveness, but she didn't want the rest of the band to come back out of the restrooms and interrupt. Especially the wizard, but in a band whose drummer was an Outcast from the Mirror Queendom and whose organ player was a sorcerer, who knew what other hidden talents and threats might lurk?

Besides, the singer Jim was amazing. He met her every attack with a parry or a sidestep, and he fought like the furniture and people around him were a third weapon constantly at his disposal. He flicked tumblers at Jane with the tips of her own knives, and kicked stools in her direction, and when a scar-faced man with a bandanna covering his shaved head—maybe a bouncer—moved to intervene, Jim tripped him and kicked him into Jane's way like he was rolling a barrel down a gangplank.

Time to take decisive action.

Jane launched her effort with a fierce counterattack, genuinely hurling herself at the singer's jugular and crotch with staggered, alternating blows. She did her best to cut his flesh, but she was unsurprised when his lightning speed and panther-like athleticism kept him out of harm's way.

Nor was she surprised when he stabbed her, sinking her blade into her belly.

She let herself go slack and stare.

The screaming of the college girls was very loud in her ears.

Jim sank the second blade into her back, between her shoulder blades. Jane felt it bite deep into her heart, and she grimaced in pain.

Jim stared at her fiercely. His lips mouthed words: "*Who are you?*" This close, she knew his face. He looked so very much like his brother.

How odd, Jane thought. How very nearly amusing.

She let the hammering pain force one of her knees to buckle, not losing contact with the big man's gaze. He caught her from falling and repeated his lips-only, silent query.

"Easy with the lady, mister," Jane heard, and in the corner of her vision she saw the bartender, John from North Carolina, arrive. He held his shotgun leveled at Jim, and the singer frowned. "I saw as it was her who attacked you first, but I reckon it's time for all the stabbin' to be wrapped up."

Jane grabbed the strapping on Jim's belly with one hand and cut at it with the knife in her other. It was duct tape, and as the tape and the object wrapped in it came away in her hand, she head-butted Jim the rock and roll singer in his handsome face.

Jim staggered back, blood spattering down his face from his nose.

John turned to object and she ran him over, knocking him to the ground with her shoulder in his midriff. Unexpectedly, a rush of feeling coursed through her. Searching her memory, she recognized it as glee. With any luck, she thought, she might be dead by morning.

And she'd take that angelic bastard with her.

She shouted the Adamic incantation of her spell as she vaulted over the bar, spraying blood on everything she touched. The crow flapped its wings and plunged into the *Wild Turkey* mirror ahead of her—

and then she jumped again, into the glass and gone on the tail of the black bird.

CHAPTER THREE

Qayna—who, millennia later, would be known as Jane—came home from her fields and found Abil waiting.

He was cleaned up, out of his customary kidskins and leggings and instead wearing a white tunic and sandals. His hair was oiled, and he smelled of flowers rather than of the herd. The whole family stood behind him, Father, Mother, Shet, the younger children. Behind the family, towering above them and crackling white, stood one of the Messengers, his six wings flapping steadily behind him as if to keep him in flight, though his feet appeared to touch the ground.

They were all waiting for her.

○ ○ ○

Qayna had been in the fields because she worked, as everyone worked. She never felt unsafe, however long she was alone—the beasts, for the most part, didn't molest her, and there were not yet any other people besides her immediate family—and she accepted the work. Her mother, though, in hushed tones when they were alone together under a comforting moon, had often told her of a time when all their kind had been only two, and there had been no such thing as work and no risk of starvation or any other kind of death, only love and tending the plants of the garden. Mother's stories of discovering the infinite variety of life and nurturing it so that it could blossom to its fullest thrilled Qayna's heart in a way she could not make Abil understand, and she tried to be like Mother in her daily tasks, her contribution to feeding and clothing the family.

Abil chose instead to work with Father. Qayna was the oldest, but Abil was second, and he was nearly Father's height and serious when the rest of the children were a gangly troop of monkeys, always on the heels of cheerful young Shet. Abil worked with the herds, which was a labor of long hours. He milked ewes, cared for injured animals, chased away wolves, sheared the flock before lambing every spring, and, when one of the herd was to die to feed the family, it was Abil who chose the animal to make the ultimate gift.

Abil's was a lonely work, and Qayna didn't envy it. Besides the long hours he spent leaning on his staff in the fields, it was Abil who moved the sheep into warmer valleys when the winter winds came. At those times, Father stayed with the family, which was good, because Father's first task was to oversee the instruction of his children.

On the same day the herds went to the winter pastures, Father would retreat into his own private tent for hours, and then the Messengers would come. Jane knew why they came, because she had crawled as a child under the tent flaps and listened to Father's rhymes, the names he had given the Messengers in them and the odd words he used to conjure them. And the summoning was not the end of Father's responsibilities; the Messengers came from the towers in the west bringing lore and learning, but it was Father's job to make sure his children were prepared and to repeat their lessons with the family over and over until they were taken fully to heart. If his children didn't learn and live the teachings of the Bearers of the Word, Father told them, then the Bearers of the Sword might come in their stead. All this was well and good, and, Qayna thought, the proper order of things.

Still, it meant long, cold nights for her brother, huddled over a small fire with his flute and his wallet of dried lambs' flesh.

Qayna, meanwhile, combed the forests and the fields for herbs that were edible, good for body and spirit, and she brought them to the family. As Father taught the children the Way and Mother whispered lessons to Qayna of the Garden, Qayna in turn taught the plants. With example, with firm, dirt-fisted persuasion, with patience and with love she taught them to stand in rows, to grow upright, to be nourishing and cheerful, and to beautify the hillsides above the family's dwellings of skin and stone. On winter nights, when her grain slept in silent furrows, waiting for the spring to rise and bud, she stooped under the lintel to return to her Father's fire in the evenings and spared a thought for her brother in the hills, a thought that was loving and compassionate.

Loving and compassionate, but nothing more.

During this most recent winter, a tall Messenger with an expressionless face taught the family about the Bond. The Bond was the tie that connected Father and Mother and all of them together, and the First Precept was that man and woman should enter into the Bond, be fruitful and multiply. Qayna had found it amazing, and though she had shushed the tittering of the younger children, she had found it embarrassing, too, and she was vaguely relieved that Abil wasn't present. But late at night, when Father and the six-winged Messenger stood on the brow of the hill and recited the names and deeds of the stars above them, Mother whispered to Qayna that it was all true.

Not only was it all true, she confirmed, but Qayna had to prepare herself. She was to be the first woman to enter into the Bond east of the Garden. This was the Way for her daughters to keep the First Precept, ever since Mother's own choice, a mysterious fork in the path to which she only alluded and only in hushed tones, but which sounded like a decision freighted with dread, rebellion, and regret.

Qayna expressed doubt.

Her body was ready, Mother explained patiently; it was time. In the same way, Qayna prepared the earth before she filled it with seed, enriching the soil with the castoffs from the family's table, so that the seed could flourish in it and grow into tall stalks of wheat or fruit trees, Qayna had been preparing her own body.

Qayna denied it.

She was outraged. She had participated in no such embarrassing pursuit, and besides, there was no one for her to marry. Would the

Messenger take a rib from her side and make a companion for her? Would he form a man from the dust for her convenience and pleasure?

Mother insisted. She had prepared her body without knowing, feeding it and exercising it and making it strong. And Qayna's body had responded; the changes in her flesh that had sent her once under each moon into Mother's private, separated tent were a clear sign that her body was ready to fulfill its purpose, to achieve the task designated for it by its creator. Mother had told the Messenger about these changes, she admitted to Qayna, and that was why the Messenger now taught the family about marriage.

Besides, the First Precept was inexorable. There was only the family, and if the family did not multiply, then there would be no more people, only a wide world, empty but for the Towers and the Messengers. And the Bond, cruel as it might seem, would tie her and a mate together for their own protection, and the protection of their children.

What children? Qayna asked. What mate?

It was time, Mother explained, and there was a companion.

There was Abil.

Qayna fled. She didn't want Abil, not as anything other than her brother. She wasn't sure about the First Precept and the Bond generally, but she knew that she wasn't ready yet, and maybe never would be. Horrified and sickened at the thought of what was proposed, angry at the base treachery of her mother, she began from that day to carry a knife.

Abil returned with the warmer weather, as green tendrils started cautiously to poke their heads out of Qayna's furrows. He was tall and worn by the weather, his jaw becoming straighter and his arms and legs longer and more muscular, like Father's. Qayna couldn't look at him directly, and neither could she avoid looking at him when she was in his presence. Mostly she tried to avoid him, dunging and pruning the orchard and the field and searching his face, when she could do so without being noticed, for any sign that he, too, had spoken with the Messenger this winter.

She wondered if he *knew*.

Shet and the others, meanwhile, seemed to follow her even more closely than they always had, giggling and pointing at her whenever she caught them peeking around a corner or peeping up from behind a rock. The little children pointed and giggled, anyway. Shet just stared.

Until the day when she came back from watering her farthest field and found the family gathered in front of their dwelling.

O   O   O

Abil stood in front of Mother and Father, perfumed and oiled. He was dressed in a fine white kilt Mother must have woven and sewn for him, and tooled sandals that had obviously been cut, stitched and dyed by Father. Her parents held up more clothing, she guessed for her, and they smiled.

Behind them rose the Messenger. He was tall, far taller than Abil or even Father, and his skin, his robe, and his six wings all glowed crackling white. His hair danced and snapped like flames in the spring breeze, and there was a smell about him that was unnatural and unearthly. He had a strong, imperious brow and piercing eyes that seemed perfectly clear and bottomless. Qayna had never felt totally at ease around this Messenger or any others of his kind, but she was especially uncomfortable now.

"Come," Mother said.

"Come," Father repeated.

Abil smiled. It was an ugly smile, a smile Qayna had never seen before on a human face, a smile that looked like it belonged on the bristling muzzle of a wolf.

"It is time," the Messenger boomed. His voice was like lightning in the far hills in Autumn, a thundered utterance that was impossible to misunderstand and that brooked no dissent.

"No!" Qayna cried, and she fled.

Qayna bathed in a spring beyond her orchard, in private and in secret. The spring was her own special place, a canyon of young stone and crystal water she had discovered while chasing fluttering spores in a dry summer storm the year before. She ran to the spring now, not directly because she feared pursuit, but by a circuitous route. She dropped below the fields into a gully, crossed a river, climbed a hill, and then finally came to her spring by traveling downstream from its sources.

She undressed, trembling from shock and rage, laying her tunic and sandals on a large rock beside the stream and setting her small knife carefully on top of them. She threw herself into the water, gasping from the sudden cold shock.

The spring was deep, and with the chill of the water prickling her skin, Qayna sank to the bottom. The solid reality of the rock beneath her bare feet and hands reassured her that the earth and its limits were unchanged, and when the pressure on her lungs became so real that it began to pain her, she surfaced.

Abil stood above her at the water's edge, and behind him waited the Messenger.

"Am I so bad then, Qayna?" Abil asked. The look on his face was petulant and wounded, a look such as Shet might wear if a prized toy had been taken away from him. Something else lurked in the expression, too, a note of violence that Abil could not entirely hide. "Am I so bad that you will not have me?"

Once Qayna and Abil would have played together freely, naked and thoughtless. Now she stayed in the water, trying to keep her body from his eyes and unable to think of anything but the strange and terrible revelations the Messenger had delivered the previous winter about Mother, Father and the First Precept. As if he were thinking of the same thing, Abil couldn't keep his eyes off her body, and stared at the water in front of her and the rippling, distorted images it bore.

"Am I a beast?" Qayna replied. There was no word for *slave* in the tongue of her birth, as there was yet no one to enslave. "Am I a mere thing that has no say in its own use? Am I a garment to be worn and cast aside, a tool with which to harrow up the earth, a lamb to be slaughtered?"

"It is the First Precept," the Messenger intoned. Between the canyon walls that enclosed the spring, his words rolled like the cracking of the heavens. He hesitated. "Do you choose to disobey the will of Heaven?"

"You would not have me choose at all!" Qayna shouted. The heat of the anger warmed her against the water's cool bite. "You would have me only lower my head and submit! That is not the joy of the Garden, that is not the path of my Mother!"

Abil crouched beside the water, beside the stone on which she had laid her things. Perhaps he meant it as a way not to appear threatening, but it brought him closer to Qayna and that felt like an invasion. Besides, squatting on his heels, he opened his tunic and exposed his body in a way that reminded Qayna uncomfortably of the fact that he, like she, was no longer a child, and that his body, too, had prepared to obey the First Precept.

"Let's choose to obey together," Abil said, grinning. "We could choose to do otherwise together, but let's choose to obey."

"Obedience is sacrifice," the Messenger trumpeted. His voice was loud and brassy, but Qayna thought she heard the faintest note of compassion in it. "To obey is to sacrifice the other things you might have done, the other possibilities you might have enjoyed. If those other possibilities were always and in all respects bad, obedience would be painless. Every commandment is a summons to obedience, a call to sacrifice on the altar."

The horrible, ineluctable tone in which the Messenger spoke, and the tiny trace of warmth in his voice, only made the content of what he said completely unacceptable, even though, Qayna realized, the words were true.

"I'm not ready!" she cried, treading water. "Not now! Can I not wait?"

"It is the First Precept," the Messenger repeated. "You must choose now." The gigantic being's voice softened considerably. "I, too, have no choice."

"Come on, Qayna," Abil splashed into the water after her. He was laughing, but Qayna didn't think there was anything to laugh about, and his mad chuckle did nothing to break the rising wall of tension in her breast.

She backed away from him, towards the edge of the spring.

"You know me. You know the Messenger's teaching, and the Way, and what Father and Mother have done." He swam towards her.

She splashed out of the water on the far side, staring down at her brother. He stared up at her, his eyes on her naked body, and now his look truly became the hungry stare of a wild animal. Qayna felt vulnerable and threatened, the more so when she realized that the Messenger was staring at her, too.

And the Messenger's eyes, always so patient and mechanical and full of rote wisdom, were now full of something else. Something animal, something that burned.

Abil splashed for the bank. He was a fast swimmer, faster than Qayna, and her heart and mind raced in fear. She ran around the edge of the water, brambles and sharp stones cutting into the work-toughened skin of her feet, running for her clothes.

"Stop!" the Messenger roared, but he didn't move to intervene.

"Stop!" Abil cried, and he sloshed out of the water on her heels.

Qayna scooped up her scant belongings in both hands and kept running. Along the bank of the spring she raced, into thickets of long-spined thorn trees that grew where the stone raced above the water higher and higher in narrow ledges and steep slopes. Abil had longer legs than she did, and heavier muscle, but she thought she was more nimble and might be able to evade him if she could get to where agility would make a difference.

Abil caught her in the trees. She dropped her clothes as her brother slammed her against a stone wall cluttered with dried tree branches. Stray thorns dug into the flesh of her belly and thighs and her blood marred the virgin rock. Though her sandals and tunic fell into the thicket, she kept possession of the knife, and as Abil pounded her against the stone again, she tightened her fingers around it.

"Stop!" the Messenger cried.

"This is the First Precept!" Abil raged, and threw his body against hers. He was awkward and animal and he approached her from behind and butted her, like a ram subdues a recalcitrant ewe.

"I …" the Messenger hesitated.

Qayna fought back with her ankles and elbows, and Abil pushed her harder against the rock.

"Obey!" he snapped wolfishly.

She wiggled around and pushed him away with both feet, feeling the rough stone abrade the skin of her back with the force of the blow. "Abil!" she cried. She was trapped by the thorn trees and the stone, and the knife in her hand seemed both pitiably small and laden with doom. "I am no beast!"

"You *must!*" Abil snarled. "It is the will of Father and Mother! It is the will of Heaven!"

"It is not *my* will!" she shouted back.

The Messenger was silent, and Abil threw himself forward—

Qayna swung the knife fiercely, aiming for Abil's chest, willing the blade to wound and subdue her brother—

but the weapon had darker plans.

The point of the small knife sank into his throat and Abil's blood gushed over her, surprisingly hot on her water- and wind-chilled body. Abil thrashed and jerked, and pulling himself off the blade only opened the wound and caused his blood to spill faster.

Qayna stared in shock as her brother, and would-be Bond mate, staggered away from her clutching at a gaping hole in his neck, fell backwards into the embrace of a tree of thorns, and crashed to the ground.

Qayna still held the knife, slick and warm. For long seconds, it was all she could do to focus her entire will on not fainting.

Slowly, she looked up at the Messenger, uncertain how he would react. The Messenger looked back at her, and in his clear, translucent eyes she saw deep reserves of will and sudden, terrible insight.

The Messenger drew himself up to his full height, like a mighty oak tree, and suddenly he opened his robe. His glowing body was even more finely-muscled than Abil's, as if it were the light and the original at the same time, and Abil's newly-acquired man-body were merely a shadow.

"And now … daughter of Eve?" the Messenger rumbled. He spoke slowly, but as he spoke he picked up speed, as if he were making up his mind. "Now what do you choose, since you have learned the unstoppable power of your own free will? You are a rebel against the First Precept. Will you rebel with me?"

Qayna fled again, scrambling through trees that clutched at her and tore her flesh. She scrambled up the stone and way, staring back at the Messenger behind her. "Who are you?" she demanded. Mother had taught her the First Precept, and though Qayna feared and rejected it, she knew that it didn't mean that the Messengers were supposed to mingle with the mortals entrusted into their care. "You defy Heaven, too!"

"I am Azazel," the Messenger called back, smiling brilliantly, "and you teach me that I need not care."

"I want nothing from you!" she cried at the terrible, naked figure.

"Remember me, mortal!" the Messenger bellowed, his rumbling voice rebounding against the sky itself.

Then Qayna tumbled out of the top of the canyon and left the Messenger Azazel behind.

○ ○ ○

She ran naked and bloody, holding nothing but the knife that had killed her brother. That night, she butchered lambs from Abil's herd and hid from the eyes of Father and Shet, who wandered the hills crying her name and Abil's. She wondered what had happened to the Messenger Azazel, and why he had not reported his own failure, or Qayna's crimes.

She traveled at night, taking comfort from the rebel moon and nursing the thought that if she was a disobedient child, she had learned from a Mother with a similar streak. By day she lay in the hollows of rocks, ate the flesh of her stolen lambs and chewed on roots she dug out of the ground. When she slept, she dreamed that the stones around her were the grinding, merciless arms of her dead brother, Abil.

On the third day, they found her.

It was Shet who was staring at her, wide-eyed, when she awoke.

"They found Abil," her younger brother said. "And your clothes."

She stood, dropping the last of the uneaten carcass and the tiny, guilty blade.

Then came Father, the sternness of his brow trembling in hint of softer feelings behind the facade, and with him a company of Messengers. She expected them to bring Swordbearers, but there were only the blue-white, six-winged giants she had always seen. She searched the faces of the Bearers of the Word—the first time she had ever really done so—wondering whether she might see Azazel and almost hoping that she would. She had witnessed terrible things in his eyes, a rage to possess and to destroy, but at least when she had looked into his eyes she had seen *something*, and not just the blank tables on which were inscribed the long list of Heaven's mandates.

But she was disappointed; Azazel was not among them.

"I'm sorry," Father grunted, grabbing her by her shoulders and throwing her down.

"I deserve it," she said. She didn't really mean it, but she hadn't intended to cause Father grief.

"This world is a hard and fallen one," he said, tears streaming down his cheeks. "That is not your fault."

The foremost of the Messengers bore down upon her, a clay pot in his hand. Qayna stared at the Messenger's face, imprinting it upon her memory. "This dye," the Messenger thundered, "is the blood of Abil. His blood cried to heaven to witness your guilt, and now it will cry to all your family and their descendants as an eternal witness."

The Messenger dipped a shard of bone into the pot and scraped its jagged edge across Qayna's face. She screamed and twisted, and Father held her down.

"This stylus is the bone of Abil," the Messenger continued. "You would not make an acceptable sacrifice, and instead sacrificed your own brother's flesh and bone. Now the bone records your sin."

The Messenger continued scratching her, running curving lines about Qayna's face and all over her body. Qayna bucked and screamed and stared at each Messenger, memorizing their faces. One day, she swore, it would be her turn to witness, and the Messengers would be the ones screaming in pain.

Father wept, but did not relent.

Shet only stared.

"These words that I write upon your face," the Messenger finished, "are all the names of Abil. "As you have blotted out his name from among your family, so shall your name be blotted out. As you have taken from him his life, so do I now take from you your death. You shall be a fugitive and a vagabond upon the earth, until the end of time."

The Messenger arose and stood away, but the pain did not subside. As Father stood and turned away also, pulling Shet with him and abandoning Qayna to her pain, she rolled over and curled into a ball, sobbing.

She lay a long time. There was no one to find her or to be disturbed.

When she was done weeping, hours had passed and her pain had subsided into a stinging that covered her entire body. She stood gingerly and picked up the bloody knife where she had dropped it. She picked it up because she needed a tool of some kind in the great empty world into which she had been cast, and she picked it up because was hungry to someday, somehow, get her revenge.

And then she saw, perched on an outcropping of stone above her, a large black crow.

CHAPTER FOUR

Millennia later, Jane leaped through the *Wild Turkey* mirror behind the bar in Wellman's.

She landed in the Outer Bounds expecting to hear its usual soft-swishing silence. Instead, the halls and arches echoed to the sounds of shouting.

"Let go of her, damn you!" The voice belonged to the guitar player, Eddie. He sounded like he was just around the corner, but Jane knew that sound could carry a long, long way in the Mirror Queendom. Especially in the Outer Bounds.

"She's an Outcast in violation of the terms of her exile!" squeaked an excited fairy voice that might have belonged to Foxtail. "You have no right to talk to the Queen's Rangers like that, and you have no permission to be here!"

"We don't need *permission*, *cagado*!" That would be Mike. "We have *guns*."

"And don't go imagining our bark is worse," the organ player snarled, "et cetera. We also have fireballs."

Jane pulled her knives from her own body, carefully wiping each on her duster before sheathing it. The hoof was as long as her forearm and looked like a gigantic toenail clipping, polished and smooth. It was the right size to be Azazel's. Of course, when she had first known him, he had had feet.

The hooves—and the wings—had been *his* mark, but they had been his own doing.

"You'll risk the wrath of Mab and Oberon," *thud!* "for *this* wretch?"

"If Mab and Oberon ain't pissed off with us already," the guitar player laughed out loud, "they're just about the only ones."

As Jane removed the blade from her heart, a sudden gush of hot fluid spilled out, but she felt the flesh of the pierced organ knit together almost instantly, and then the wound shut and the blood stopped. An ancient ward kept any of her blood from staining the duster, so it dripped onto the floor instead.

She took the shell-rigged-into-a-makeshift-vial from her pocket, removed the wax and poured the blob of quicksilver out into her palm.

BOOM!

The sound of an explosion deafened Jane for a moment, and shock waves knocked her against the wall. When she stood again, moments later, she could hear animal yelps, the scrabbling of paws on stone and a pair of running feet.

"Twitch!" Eddie hollered. "We're on!"

"You think I care about the *show?*" Twitch called back. "I'm going to kick that bitch in the forehead!"

The wizard muttered something Jane couldn't hear.

"Are you sure?" Eddie asked.

"Go!" Adrian yelled.

Then the pair became a crowd of feet, and the rattling hoof beats of a horse.

Jane incanted in Adamic and followed the silver bead in her palm. Its movements were subtle enough that she had to keep an eye on the wiggling drop, and couldn't rely on her sense of touch alone. Staring into her own cupped hand slowed her, but even worse was the fact that the bead led her backward, straight into the teeth of her pursuit.

Wondering how many fey eyes had already examined her and seen what she was carrying, Jane slid the hoof into the inside pocket of her duster. She pinned it with her elbow against her side to keep it secure, and drew the pistol.

The gun was an FN Model 1910, a mediocre old semi-automatic pistol at best, vintage turn of the twentieth century. This particular pistol, though, was unique. Its serial number was 19074. It had been purchased by the Black Hand and its owner, the Serbian enthusiast Gavrilo Princip, had taken it at midnight, on June 27, 1914, to a shadowy crossroads outside Sarajevo. There a *veštica* with the face of a young girl but the hands of a crone had anointed the gun with boiled fat extracted from the body of a murdered priest and pronounced over the weapon a dreadful curse.

Jane had been watching from the shadows.

The next day, young Princip had killed the Habsburg Archduke Franz Ferdinand with this same pistol, and started World War I. The gun, famous to those who followed it as the Calamity Horn, was a killer of kings; that was its blessing, and the purpose for which Princip had wanted it. There was no creature its bullets could not wound, Angelic or Infernal, cursed or anointed.

It could even wound Jane. But it couldn't, as she found out on the third day after the veštica had done her work, kill her. Not even with a bullet through the temple. So all Jane's tedious labor in training the veštica and in nurturing the nationalistic madness in young Gavrilo had gone to waste. Her scheme to end her life had failed, and instead millions of others had died.

The madness that the gun caused was, apparently, an unintended side effect of the witch's enchantment.

The quicksilver bead in her palm tugged Jane to the right into a square room several paces across, with a circular shaft in the center of the chamber and a ceiling that was so far away it was invisible. At the same moment that Jane saw the bead, she heard the horse clatter into the room in front of her. She looked up and fired three quick shots.

Bang! Bang! Bang!

The echoes were infinite and deafening, a wave of sound that crashed out of the cursed gun and blasted along the passageways in all directions. The horse reared in surprise and went down in a tangle of hooves and wings and bright-splattering blood.

Right behind the horse rushed in the three rock and roll musicians, and the wave of sound struck them full in the face. For a moment, they seemed to hang suspended in mid-air and their faces contorted with sudden insight and anger.

Then Mike turned, raised his pistol—

and fired on his companions.

Eddie ducked, roared and fired back.

Jane veered right, skirting around the pit at her feet. Out of the corner of her eye, she saw movement within the pit, the rustling, quaking tremble of many-limbed things that were climbing inside, but then she was past it and gone.

"Selenen abiuro!" Adrian shouted, throwing a pocketful of ground and powdered something into the air—

Jane smelled an herb that might have been oregano—

Mike and Eddie dropped their guns, horrified looks on their faces—

and Adrian himself collapsed to the ground, unconscious.

Jane fled the room at a run, gun pointed at the ceiling and hoof under her arm. The Model 1910's magazine held seven rounds, which left her only three shots. Really, she had not been thrifty with her ammunition. One shot would have been enough to induce madness in the rock and rollers, and the only reason she had fired more was the presence of the fairy.

The gun's bullets injured fairies and could kill them, but its sound did nothing to their minds. This, Jane guessed, was because fairies were already insane.

A net struck her, flung from a passage to her right, and bowled Jane sideways. The snare was woven of something elastic and slightly sticky, and weighted with what looked like giant acorns. Under the force of the attack, Jane slipped to her knees, but she managed to avoid dropping anything.

"What is it, what is it, a big ugly outsider!" Three thin-bodied persons in leather armor sprang from a shadowed alcove and raced in a circle around Jane, shaking wooden spears over their heads. One had a skunk's tail and coloring, one a monkey's, and a third kept shifting back and forth between a humanoid shape and the shuffling, wheezing form of a small brown bear. "Outsider, topsider, flat-worlder!" they chanted, not in unison. "Big-footed, ugly, smelly human!"

Beyond them, the crow settled onto a head-sized knob at the bottom of a staircase banister and glared at her.

Jane listened and thought she could hear Adrian chanting. Whatever had knocked the wizard out, his friends had him awake again, and he was probably dealing with Twitch's injury. She also heard the pounding of many feet, and flapping wings.

Dragging the weight on her shoulders, Jane stood. The three fairies stopped and staggered back at the sight of her.

"Do you not know me?" Jane demanded slowly. "I am the Marked Woman."

A horse whinnied behind Jane, in the maze of the Outer Bounds. The fairies before her slipped away, fear and embarrassment on their faces.

"We're the Queen's Rangers!" Brown Bear gruffed.

"Vengeance rides in my wake," Jane added, beginning to get irritated, "sevenfold and hungry." She shook the net with her hand and found that the fibers clung to her skin and the fabric of her duster and hat.

"We can't!" Skunk squealed. "We can't do it!"

The fairy raised his tail in excitement and his comrade Brown Bear grabbed it and yanked it back down with a look of warning on his face. "Duty!"

"Release me," Jane said flatly, "or die." She heard the horse Twitch coming after her again.

The fairies scattered. "It's spider silk!" Monkey called over her shoulder as she scrambled under an archway no bigger than a cupboard door. "We can't release you! You're stuck until it melts!"

Jane muttered in Adamic and poured her ka into the spider silk net, burning it instantly into ash. She strode forward in the falling curtain of cinders, regretting the low, drained state to which she had reduced her ka and kicking herself for having been caught in an ambush set by fairies, of all creatures.

Gunfire erupted behind her, but her ears didn't pick up the popping and snapping of bullets passing her, so she guessed the shots must be coming from the guns of the rock and roll band, and they must not be shooting at her.

The fairies were attacking them, too.

She picked up the pace, jogging. She was surprised and a little annoyed at how long it was taking her to get to her destination, though of course distance on earth and distance in the Mirror

Queendom bore no correlation to each other. She wondered if she might have been better off just running out the front of Wellman's in ordinary mortal space, but cut off the line of self-doubt immediately. She'd had no way of guessing the rock and rollers would be this persistent, and once she shook them, passage through the Outer Bonds would be a good first step to shaking off pursuit. Besides, she hadn't been foolish enough to leave her ride in front of the road-house.

It occurred to her that it was strange that they were following her. Maybe Twitch wanted revenge for the pain and humiliation Jane had inflicted on her. But was it possible that the band somehow realized she had the hoof, and were chasing her to get it back? Could they have communicated with Jim somehow?

Jane holstered the Calamity Horn and pulled the hoof from her pocket. Examining it slowed her pace, but running forward into unknown peril was a fool's choice, and the band seemed occupied with the Queen's Rangers anyway.

The hoof was curved like a crescent moon, wide as two of Jane's fingers and thick as one. It was yellowish in the light of the Outer Bounds, odorless and smooth like ivory, like a stone worn from millennia of lying in a river bed.

Except, Jane's fingers found with practiced probing, for one tiny little chip.

Either the power that had smoothed the hoof fragment out— the waters of Dudael, Jane guessed, having been there recently and seen the holding pit of her one-time conflicted antagonist—had missed a tiny divot, or since the hoof's extraction from the waters, someone had cut from the inside a tiny flake, a chip the size of her own pinky's nail.

Which could be how they were following her.

Jane cursed, her words of annoyance shaking dust from the lintel of a doorway under which she passed and sending a scuttling thing like an orange centipede scurrying for cover. She sent some of her precious reserves of ka-force over the clipping where her fingers had been, searching for the connection she guessed must exist—

and there it was. Jane felt it with her ka like a ribbon of water, tenuous, subtle and invisible, stretching away into the maze behind

her. It must be the wizard Adrian, she guessed. These thieves feared
other criminals, and so they had taken measures to allow them to
track the hoof if anyone stole it from them.

She considered briefly how this impacted her plan and decided
that it was a good thing. The more noise these loose cannons of rock
and roll made, the more likely they were to attract the renegade, which
was all Jane cared about. The band was nothing to her, the hoof was
nothing, even Azazel was nothing; she just wanted to carry out the
task appointed by the Legate and get her reward.

And kill Raphael.

The crow flapped ahead of her in the maze.

It wheeled in front of two figures, who waited before a window
in the wall the size of a ladies' compact mirror, or the rear view
mirror of a motorcycle. They stood tall, straight-backed and regal.

Jane put the hoof away and drew the Horn.

"You travel cloaked in myth," one of the figures smiled gently.
She was a tall, thin woman with pale skin, long hair like spun gold
and a crown of oak leaves on her head. She wore a green gown and
green slippers the color of dew-spattered grass.

"I bought the coat in Sydney," Jane said. "You supposed to be
Mab, then?"

"Am I?" the Queen arched an eyebrow. "Australia is a long way
from Kansas, in mortal space." The waves of her efforts to seduce
Jane splashed around them all and rebounded off the walls, but Jane
was unmoved. It was like smelling rotting meat—she couldn't miss
the stink, and she certainly didn't want to take a bite, however widely
the person offering it might grin. Even without the quicksilver in her
palm, Jane was resistant to the charm of the fey folk, but with it, she
was immune. "But I see you travel as one of us."

Jane shrugged. "I get around."

"You must be tired." These words came from her companion,
a man of the same height, with jet black hair and an identical crown.
"Why don't you rest with us? I'm sure we have a lot to share." He
was also dressed in green, in a tailed coat and velvety green trousers
and he, too, stank of seduction like fly-blown meat.

"Let me pass."

"You are the Marked Woman." Now his voice sounded
wheedling and, ever so slightly, uneasy.

"So that gives you a hint as to why your Glamour doesn't affect me. It should also tell you that you really ought to get out of my way," Jane said. It was hard to be certain, but she thought the gunfire was getting closer. She didn't want to fight, if she could avoid it. The fairies in front of her didn't have visible tails, and each wore a leather belt with a sword hanging from it.

"You are in my lands now," the Queen said.

"More or less," Jane grunted. She turned the pistol so the fairies could get a clearer view of it.

The King nodded solemnly. "As she said, you travel cloaked in legend."

"I don't want to kill you," Jane said, "but I won't have my hand forced."

"You would murder Queen Mab on her own doorstep?" the Queen looked affronted, staring at Jane down her long nose. "Queen Mab and her consort Oberon, Peerless Among the Fey?"

Jane laughed and swore in Adamic. The curse word shook the mirror hanging behind the two fairies askew. "Maybe," she said, "and maybe not." Behind her, she definitely heard the sound of fighting getting louder. "You can't kill me, and I have no people you can retaliate against. Why should I hesitate at the thought of killing Mab?"

"If the occupants of the Mirror Throne were crassly murdered by a Flatworlder," the Queen sniffed, "there would be war between the worlds. Are you so detached from your father's and mother's descendants that you can accept that?"

Jane shrugged her shoulders. "Maybe," she said again, "and maybe not. But I'd sure as *hell* kill a couple of Queen's Rangers stupid enough to dress up in costume and try to fool me. And nobody would go to war over that."

They didn't blink. The King curdled his eyebrows like she'd said something distasteful. "Queen's *Rangers?*" he sneered.

She pointed the gun at him. "Drop your pants," she ordered.

He sneered and did nothing.

Pop! Pop! Whizzang!

The sudden presence of bullets in the air told Jane that the band had caught up to her and she was out of time. If her ka weren't so drained, or her pistol, she'd turn and fight them. On the other hand, if her resources were less exhausted, she could have just blasted these annoying fairies into oblivion. Instead, she raised the pistol and fired a shot into the air.

Bang!

"Two left," she said, pointing the muzzle at Oberon. "I don't miss."

"Stop!" he pleaded, his eyes suddenly serious.

"Oberon …" the Queen warned him.

With quick but trembling fingers, the King undid his belt buckle and dropped his green pants into a velvety puddle around his pointy-toed shoes. A donkey's tail twitched nervously into sight.

"I thought so." *Bang! Bang!* Jane emptied the Model 1910, firing the last two shots into the center of the fake Oberon's chest. He flew back without a sound, hitting the wall and sinking to the floor.

"Give my regards to Mab," Jane snorted. She stepped past the surviving fairy chanting in Adamic, burning nearly the last of her ka-fire in the act.

The gate opened and she flowed into it, her whole body passing through the window, tiny though it was.

"Stop her!" she heard at her back, but then the fracas and the Outer Bounds were gone. The crow, of course, followed her through.

The night outside Dodge City, Kansas, was cool and clear, with a thick cloud cover blocking out the stars overhead. Jane stepped out of the mirror, turned, and plucked it from the saddle strap to which it had been clipped. She dashed it on the roadside gravel. To be sure, she ground it into even smaller shards with her heel.

She had other mirrors with her, but it would take the wizard Adrian longer to find them.

"Easy, girl," she said.

She stood several miles away from Wellman's, at the bottom of the bank below the highway and at the edge of an endless field of sorghum. The bushy grass waved cheerfully at her in the darkness, and before she did anything else, Jane stopped and reloaded the Calamity Horn. She filled the clip with thirty-two caliber Auto rounds and then holstered the gun. The shells were unimpressive, weak as far as modern handgun ammunition went—the gun and its curse were everything.

At the right end of the sorghum field was a two-pump gas station, closed for the night, but automatic pumps and vending machines still meeting the needs of one customer in a red pick-up truck. At the left end was a boxy brick building, the sign at the front of which read *FINE CUTS, INC.*

Jane swung into the saddle easily, though the horse—the Mare—was enormous. The Mare, not domesticated and not friendly but accustomed to bearing Jane, curled back its lips to reveal sharp, feline teeth and pranced sideways a step. The Mare smelled of sweaty beast and smoke; she always did. She snorted thickly in acknowledgement of her rider and Jane snorted back. The Mare was the last of the horses of Diomedes, a brutal, bullish man rumored to have been one of the many sons of the profligate Semyaz. The others had been killed centuries ago by an aimless scoundrel whom minstrels had turned into the hero Herakles. This one seemed to be immortal, and she was a fighter; the Mare would eat other animals, but her favorite food was human flesh.

Like Jane, the Mare traveled in disguise. The wards of seeming on her insured that to any casual passerby she appeared as a long, black, growling motorcycle.

"Come on, girl," Jane patted the huge horse and whistled to the animal to calm it. She pulled a fresh vial from one of the saddlebags and poured her drop of quicksilver into it, tamping it shut and replacing it in her pocket. She checked the hoof to be certain it was secure, then clucked with her tongue and pulled the Mare's reins to turn her around.

"Come on, girl," she said again and headed in the direction of the meat packing plant.

CHAPTER FIVE

Jane rode once around the meat packing plant to be sure there were no cars parked on its asphalt skirt, cracked and riddled with potholes. Early in the morning, no doubt, there would be trucks and men to load them with butchered carcasses to be shipped off, a piece here and a piece there, to grocers and restaurants in Amarillo, Oklahoma City, and Wichita. By then, Jane hoped to be finished and gone.

And maybe dead.

She had no way to detect the renegade Raphael, but she guessed that he must be close, and would come quickly when she called.

Jane would have preferred to stave in the door of the plant by arcane means, but her ka was drained and weak. Under the crow's humorless stare, she instead wrapped the Calamity Horn in a saddle blanket to muffle it and shot the lock off the back door. Inside the packing plant, she hit the light switches and looked around while she reloaded.

She stood in a small entry area with pegs on one wall heavy with lined white smocks like lab coats, red hard hats and gloves. Signs reminded employees to wear safety gear and shoes with good soles, and to punch out for any break longer than ten minutes. Human resources gibberish festooned much of the space, and there was one small office with a window that looked into the entry, dominated by a single desk and a horde of pencil stubs.

Too small for her purposes.

Jane passed into the main chamber of the plant, leading the Mare by the reins. The big room was refrigerated, and she pulled her duster closer across her chest against the cold as she looked around at a forest of cattle carcasses. The meat hung headless and shoulders down on hooks in snaking lines, from a door in the corner where Jane assumed the live cows were brought to be punched in the head, along conveyer belts where the meat was cut open and organs were removed and sorted, and finally ended in a thick grove of frozen chests that were fully prepared, and cardboard boxes full of organs and limbs, by a rolling cargo bay door.

The space was big enough for the renegade to move around in without immediately exiting. It gave Jane some cover, and limited entrances to have to watch.

The staircase up to the roof was wedged into a corner of the building between a supply closet and the back of the office. Jane hitched the Mare to a column within reach of plenty of good, if chilly, grazing, and climbed to the top alone.

A light rain was beginning to fall, and the wind picked up, threatening to rip away Jane's hat as it gusted to storm levels. Jane scanned the horizon, noting the small clump of lights that was Dodge City—and Wellman's, just at its outer edge—and the strip of shadow that was the highway, cutting among farm houses, tractor repair shops and a saddler's on its way into town. That was the direction from which the rock and roll band would come, if they really could follow the hoof and they chose to come after her.

Maybe, knowing who she was, they would give up.

The crow cut, swooping, across her vision, becoming visible in the darkness for a moment by virtue of the light it blocked out.

"Still you," Jane said. "Always you. Well, not for long."

The Legate had offered Jane a flare-scroll to get the renegade's attention, but Jane had declined. Such a device would only alert her prey that he was hunted, and she knew how to contact the Messengers. It was a skill she had learned from her Father—though not one he'd ever meant to teach her.

Her ka was beginning to recover from her exertions at the bar and in the Outer Bounds. It wasn't much, but it should be enough—

she needed very little. The rooftop itself was covered with gravel, which made it a poor surface for her purposes; the little rocks would make it impossible to draw an unbroken circle. There was a big metal box that housed a generator, though, or something to do with the building's power system. Jane chuckled at the lightning bolt decals on the side of the device, took a Sharpie from her pocket and drew a careful circle, three feet across, on top of the case. Around the outside of the circle she drew a second, meticulously inking in a line that was tidy, perfect, and steadily parallel to the inner one. She filled the space between with Adamic words—a name, single repeated over and over again, and words of calling.

When she was done she climbed atop the box and stood inside the circle. The wards themselves, the words and the circle, generated power, and she rested a moment within them, feeling the warmth as her ka slightly replenished itself. For a moment she was tempted to wait, to sit within such a circle and restore her depleted reserves.

She had been waiting six thousand years; couldn't she wait another day?

But Mab's folk knew what she had, she thought, and they wanted it. And the rock and roll band, ragged and disorganized though its members were, was tenacious and motivated and had proved to hold more than one surprise for Jane. It might hold others still, and it would be coming after her and the hoof.

And fundamentally, she thought, fixing her eye on the black bird that had dogged her vision down the millennia, she didn't *want* to wait any longer. With the Calamity Horn at her side, she didn't think she needed to.

Jane raised her arms and began to chant, not in Adamic, but in Angelic. She knew fragments of the language, in the way that modern American kids all knew oddments of Spanish, because it had been in the air, part of the environment of her childhood. These specific words, the ones she now incanted, were a rhyme she had heard Father repeat every winter, many, many years ago.

Jane's plan was simple. She would summon the renegade Messenger, and when he appeared, she would kill him. Just as she had wanted for a long, long time.

Recently, Heaven had come around to agreeing with her.

o   o   o

Three days earlier, sitting in a slowly-cooling bubble bath, Jane had realized that she was paralyzed.

She had smelled the candle smoke in the same moment, with its thick reek of cinnamon and blood, but it was too late to do anything about it. The Legate paced slowly into her hotel room. He held the candle in his hand, its flame sputtering red like a Fourth of July sparkler.

He wore red, as befitted his office. He was dressed at least a century out of style, even for one holding his office, in a half-cape-like mantelletta over white sleeves, and a broad circular galero that almost looked like Jane's own hat, though with a flail-like tail. The similarity in their outfits only repulsed Jane; she wore her hat and duster for utility, and this man wore his garb as a statement of affection for the past.

Jane had lived through the past—nearly all of it there was that a human being could claim to have experienced—she remembered it well, and she felt no longing for it. What she wanted was to move forward, to move on.

The Legate smiled an ageless smile, raised his red candle in one hand and drew out a folded piece of parchment with the other. From where she sat, Jane could see the red sealing wax on the parchment, imprinted with the image of a pair of crossed keys. "I hold a letter," he said, in a voice that was both withered and greasy, like a three-day-old hot dog on a gas station counter.

Jane looked to be sure that the Calamity Horn sat on a hand towel beside the bathtub, in easy reach if she were able to move. Not that she'd need that for the Legate—as far as she could tell, he was a mortal man, though the crow seemed bothered by his presence. The bird had flapped to the furthest corner of the Las Vegas hotel room immediately on the Legate's entrance and had stayed there since. It looked resolutely out the window, like it couldn't bring itself even to acknowledge the Legate's presence.

Nor was she worried that the Legate would steal the gun. Its original enchantment bound it to Jane's will and person, and anyone who fired it without her consent would find it a mediocre handgun, old and small. Jane had murdered the priest whose rendered fat had provided the curse-bearing anointing, and it was Jane's will that activated the terrible, murderous enchantment of the Calamity Horn. He might grab it and run, but she would get it back.

"Fine," Jane said. "I hold a knife." It was true, but it was also a bluff, inasmuch as she couldn't move her limbs or raise the blade that rested in the water under her fingers. She did have emergency resources available if she had to draw on them, but she hoped it didn't come to that.

She didn't waste time wondering how the Legate had found her or gotten into her hotel room—he was the agent of a great power, and he had means.

Besides, she was almost enjoying this soak, with the raised bathtub right in the middle of the suite and the panoramic windows over the lights of the Strip, and she was determined that the man's presence wasn't going to destroy her evening.

The Legate sank with aplomb onto the corner of Jane's bed. He set the candle on the stand beside the mattress and crossed his hands on his own lap, still holding the letter. Maybe, Jane reflected, he wore the mantelletta and the hat to give him more bulk—he was a thin man, to the point of being bony, and Jane calculated she could easily lift him over her head and throw him. He might be self-conscious; a man's size could limit his ability to exercise his charisma.

"The contents of this letter might be of interest to you," he suggested.

That introduction guaranteed that Jane wouldn't let on that she cared at all. "You're fancy, for a mailman," she teased the Legate. "Though I don't see your patch for the National Association of Letter Carriers."

"You show very little deference for the Legate of Heaven," the man frowned. He had a faint accent, which Jane thought might be Lebanese or Armenian or Hittite. She wondered where Heaven had found this man. He dressed a bit like a Cardinal, but that was mere fashion. He might be a rabbi by background, or a Sikh, or a Qodesh of Asherah. He wore wooden beads on a long string around his neck, but they were beads only, not bearing any other ornament. He thumbed slowly in a circle around the beads with his hands, and Jane saw a tattoo on the back of one hand that might be a picture of a tree, or a many-armed candlestick. "I was warned, but the extent of your indifference surprises me still."

"You people cursed me," Jane pointed out. She could have said it bitterly, but the centuries had pounded the emotional vehemence out her. The facts were the facts, and she endured. "*Indifference* isn't the word I'd choose to describe my feelings. You're lucky I don't kill you right where you sit, with a knife in the eye."

"This letter," the Legate continued, "contains the release of your judgment. It contains your forgiveness."

That caught Jane's attention, but she let no hint of her interest slip.

"This letter contains your death."

Jane trembled, slightly, from the neck up. "Sounds all right to me," she allowed. "Why don't you leave it on the table there, and help yourself to something from the minibar on the way out?"

"Forgiveness isn't free," the Legate shook his head like he had just discovered this terrible truth for himself. "Not for sins as serious as yours." He slowly licked his fingers and snuffed the candle. "But I'm pleased that you're willing to talk."

"Now's the time to hit me up," Jane chuckled to hide her relief at being able to move again, drawing her heels up to her buttocks in the deep, bubble-capped water. She wasn't afraid of death—she longed for it—but she hated being told what to do, and imposed paralysis was someone else telling her what to do. "I put down some mad dogs for the State of Nevada last week and then I hit it big on the Cockroach Road. What do you want, a hundred grand?" Money didn't matter to her, so Jane either had it in buckets or had none at all. She couldn't starve to death and paid no utility bills and the Mare could catch her own provender, so when Jane got money, she spent it. Eat, drink and be merry, might have been her motto, for tomorrow you will certainly not die.

"An eye for an eye," the Legate intoned. "A tooth for a tooth."

"A death for a death," Jane shot at him, and now she did feel bitter. "So why not kill me and get it over with?" Suddenly, she felt the full weight of the millennia at her back, and her heart filled with the pangs of the hundred cities that had burned around her and the thousands of men who had died on her blades. She was tired, she was unspeakably old, and she just … kept … *going*.

"You lost your death when you took your brother's life from him," the Legate said dryly, as if she didn't remember. He picked up the candle and tucked it into some hidden pocket beneath his mantelletta.

"What, then?" Jane asked, but in her heart she knew where the conversation was going. She willed herself not to look to the side at the Calamity Horn.

"You can have your death back," the Legate finished, shaking the letter gently like it was a birthday present and he was weighing it to guess what might be inside, "in exchange for the death of another."

"Why don't you do it yourselves?" Jane asked. "You guys aren't exactly averse to smiting, when you get the idea you'd like to do it. Ainok, Sodom and Gomorrah, Atlantis, Pompeii, San Francisco, New Orleans … why not strike this guy with a good old-fashioned thunderbolt, or a plague?"

She knew the answer, but she wanted the Legate to say it.

"This is a case where discretion will be necessary," the Legate said slowly. "Heaven would rather not attract any attention."

Jane shook soap off her hand. "And you came to me," she said, picking up the FN Model 1910, "because of my reputation for great discretion. Also, because I carry the Calamity Horn, a gun that is capable of wounding and striking down even the children of Heaven. And also because you have something you can hold over me. Here I am in Las Vegas, and Heaven is making me an offer I can't refuse."

The Legate nodded. "All true. And also, we came to you because the target in question is an old friend of yours."

O O O

On the rooftop of the meat packing plant, standing on top of the lightning bolt-bearing case, Jane raised her arms to the roiling sky and called the Messenger. Angels didn't have true names, not in the way humans did, because the ka, the *ba*, and the body of an angel were not separate things, needing a name to bind them together and casting a shadow over the space among them. An angel was a unitary creation, a spiritual point rather than a cluster, and it had no secret name. Therefore, she couldn't compel it; so instead, she invited it.

Jane called in Angelic when she could remember the Angelic words clearly, and when she couldn't, she supplied the deficit with Adamic. The two were kissing cousins, anyway, and often shared vocabulary—though Angelic, as far as Jane knew, had no profanity at all. So much the poorer.

She touched the fragment of Azazel's hoof and let the feel of the object drift into and seal her message with its tangibility. She spoke words of offer and negotiation in her incantation, telling the renegade that she had the thing he was looking for, that they could join forces, that together they could have what they both wanted.

They were lies, and a trick, and in her heart she planned murder.

The circle carried her words up into the heavens, soaring through and against the rain that pelted down. Lightning flashed in a chain along the horizon as she finished, and a vortex of silver in the dark clouds absorbed her false oaths, sucked them in and spun them out in all directions like meteorites slung at the far corners of the world.

When she was certain the angel would hear, Jane stopped. Her ka ached within her and her body's wounds, still in the final stages of healing, itched and stung. She dropped her arms and stepped down to the gravel rooftop, duster rustling and hat pounding like a drum from the fat raindrops.

The crow flapped its wings as if irritated at what she had done, and glared at her balefully. If a flesh and blood bird had given her such a look, she would have cursed at it and blown all its feathers off.

A car approached on the highway now, and Jane stepped forward and crouched at the edge of the roof to watch. Light poles were few and far between on this stretch of road, but the vehicle slowed as it passed underneath one, in front of the saddler's, and she got a clear look at it. It was a brown van, hammered as only the van of a bottom-feeding rock and roll band can be, and she knew instantly who was inside. She was impressed, though, that they'd caught up with her so quickly. The van killed its speed and then its lights, and then it disappeared in the shadow of a small copse of trees.

She needed Azazel's hoof to bait the trap for the renegade angel, but that was surely what the band must be after. Jane considered her course of action for brief seconds, and then jogged down the stairs.

She needed to hurt them, slow them down, keep them out from under her feet. And she had no fire left in her ka.

The Mare stayed where she had hitched it, razor teeth bloodied by its contented grazing on chilled beef. She pulled the beast away, earning an irascible snort of protest, but no more—decades ago, she and the animal had had it out over which one of them was to be mistress, and they both knew that Jane was the rider and the Mare was her mount.

She left the lights in the plant on. If the band really was following the hoof, they wouldn't believe she was still in the building. But maybe, if she left the lights on, the band would *think* she was trying to lure them into an ambush. That might at least keep them off balance.

She led the Mare out the back door of the plant and swung into the saddle easily. She kicked the beast into a canter and headed for the edge of the lot, where the boundary between the meat packing plant parking lot and a furrowed field of tall, storm-quaking sorghum was marked by a rail fence.

The Mare easily jumped the fence, plunging into the tall cultivated grass without fear or hesitation. Jane watched the road as she progressed, trying to spot the musicians' van—trees cut across her field of vision ahead of her, shading a lane through the planted space, and she thought a creeping darker-than-dark mass under the trees might be the van. Whoever was driving, slow as they were going, must have great night vision. Jane bent low over the Mare's neck and looked for an appropriate tool.

She found it quickly, where the crops gave way to a flat, hard aisle of dirt. There was a medium-sized tractor, and the sight of it gave her momentary pause.

It had been several millennia since she had tilled the soil, but the scent of a moist, broken clod, or the sharp, fertile promise of a gleaming agricultural tool, still pierced her to the center of her heart. For an instant she was again Qayna of the young earth, who loved plants and taught them to love her back. The tall sorghum grass could have been the barley or emmer of her youth, and under the clouds and rain the land around her could have been practically anyplace, including the valleys to the east of Eden.

A flash of lightning on the horizon, and an answering glint in the trees ahead that might have been a reflection on metal, brought her back to herself.

Jane dismounted beside the tractor, whistling to the Mare an instruction to stand in place. She unscrewed the gas cap on the tractor's tank and soaked a spare shirt in the flammable liquid. Tearing the gas-reeking cloth in half, she stuffed one half into the open tank, letting it drape wetly down the side of the tractor. The other half she wrapped around a fist-sized rock she picked up off the ground.

Through the glass of the tractor's cab, she saw the brown van pull to a stop under the gloom of the trees. Its door opened and men piled out.

It was then that she spotted the raptor that could only be Twitch, the silver falcon with the long, incongruous horse's tail trailing behind it, soaring above the trees and headed in her direction. Her wards of seeming and dissembling should hide the truth from the fairy at least for a moment, but Jane knew she needed to hurry.

She repeated her *stay* whistle to the Thracian Mare, wedged Azazel's hoof fragment firmly beneath the saddle, and retreated to the sorghum, holding in her hand the gasoline-soaked rag wrapped around a rock.

Stepping a cubit's length into the sea of grass, she pulled out a cigarette lighter and waited.

The Mare stood calmly beside the tractor, ignoring the thick reek of gasoline and the band. That was a reflection of the Mare's impressive discipline, and her centuries of training—her sense of smell was so acute that she had led Jane across three States on the trail of the brown Dodge van and never lost the scent. The falcon overhead cried angrily, and the Mare ignored that, too.

Jane drifted a couple of yards to one side to get a better view; at a fence on the far side of the dirt aisle, she saw the rock and rollers climbing into the field.

The men all carried weapons, and they approached the tractor with deliberate steps, fanning out like the fingers of a groping hand. Even in the storm-confused dim light of night, Jane could see that Adrian was in the middle of the line, holding some kind of machine pistol in one hand and looking down into the palm of his other. Jim walked beside him, sword drawn. Mike and Eddie came forward on the wings, holding pistols.

She knew that what they saw must be the tractor, and beyond it, a parked motorcycle. Then the wizard hissed something and they all halted. He dug into a pocket and came out with a piece of glass that he held up to one eye like a monocle.

"Son of a bitch!" he spat.

Jane raised the lighter to the gas bomb in her hand—
and the sky exploded into flame.

CHAPTER SIX

Qayna raced under the spires of Ainok as the trails of flame hurtled earthward. She knew that each burning meteorite, bright despite the noon sun overhead and dragging behind it a plume of black and yellow smoke, must be a Swordbearer. She should be hurrying to get out of the city, she knew, but instead she ran toward its center.

She wanted to warn Azazel; she owed him that much.

The crow flew on ahead, just beyond her reach.

Other Ainokites heeded the more sane imperative, though, and she struggled to push through them. Women and men of her own kind—not quite her own kind, but her kin, at least—rushed in a thick and burbling stream toward the gates of the city, and she had to push fiercely to force them to part and let her upstream.

The Fallen were fewer, easier to see and avoid, but much more dangerous. They towered above their mortal subjects, and though Qayna had become accustomed to their appearance, the beast heads and limbs were still terrifying when they rushed at her at full speed. A towering Fallen with the lower body of a horse, Ezeq'el, trampled people who might have been her servants, or even her lovers; a giant with the face of an octopus or a squid dragged shrieking bodies with him as he plunged into one of Ainok's great canals, finding it a more expedient route to the exits; a corpulent man with long yellow tusks jutting from his face and spikes growing from his back and shoulders lowered his head and charged through the crowd, leaving behind him a trail of mangled corpses and blood.

These were Qayna's people now, and they were destroying themselves in their flight.

The towers of Eden, Mother had told her, were observatories. She and Father had climbed within them to the platforms at their heights to watch the Messengers in flight above them, when they had been Eden's lord and lady. The spires of Ainok, for the most part, were merely spikes, but they were enormous, fingers jabbed in accusation at the sky or daggers pointed at the throat of heaven. Their heights were not platforms—other than on the one, central tower—they were the sharp points of spears.

Whether it had something to do with the spires or not, the Bearers of the Sword burned in their inexorable paths toward points outside the city.

At Ainok's center were the Grand Plaza, the Palace and the Tower. The Plaza was a wide space where the Fallen gathered to debate and, when the Council could not reach peaceable decisions, to shed each other's blood. The Palace sprawled along its western edge, all white stairs and green rooftop garden and blue water; the central source of Ainok's canals were the mighty springs beneath Azazel's home, and they burst forth from the mouths of statues of mutilated Messengers, irrigating the many acres of his private garden-like Palace before radiating out in all directions into the city. The Tower, higher, Azazel boasted, than any of the towers he had left behind, was solid inside and had an enormous staircase winding up around the outside of it to the broad circular platform at its apex.

The Plaza, the Palace, and the Tower were all made of the same gleaming white stone, not native to the hills surrounding the city. Azazel had told her once that he summoned the stone with his sorcery, from a quarry thousands of miles away. Somewhere, there was a gaping hole in a mountainside that sparkled white. The center of the city, even more than the rest of Ainok, was liberally speckled with mirrors. These were the gates of Mab's people, who were not residents but who came and went freely, and trafficked with Ainok's citizens. Azazel hadn't built the city center with wizardry, though, or with the help of the fey folk; Azazel's slaves had done the work. For himself and his own subjects, Azazel insisted on freedom. The followers of Heaven and its Messengers, he insisted, had already chosen slavery and deserved no better. Now the white stone ran red with blood, shed by slaves and citizens alike, trampled under the feet of their Fallen overlords.

Women streamed from the Palace as if its bowels also concealed a spring of concubines. Qayna drew her knife, a weapon almost long enough to call a sword, and fended the rushing women aside. Some of the women—fey or sorceresses, and in that moment Qayna envied them both—leaped into mirrors and disappeared. Those who couldn't rushed down the avenues toward the fires.

Qayna saw Azazel standing atop his Tower. The leader of the Fallen was majestic, even though the animal parts he had grafted onto himself with his own hand, and something else, some streak of wrongness, prevented him and all his kind from being truly *beautiful*. His goat-like legs were crooked, but he held his back erect, and the crimson- and black-streaked fur of his lower half was clean and shone in the sun. His wings, only two of them, were now the wings of an enormous bat, but they still cloaked him with something like majesty. He stood tall and looked about him at the horizon as the Swordbearers touched down.

So he knew. But he wasn't running.

Qayna cupped her free hand around her mouth and yelled up at him. "Azazel!"

The former Messenger looked her way instantly, and laughed a laugh like rolling thunder. He spread his wings like flexing arms, snapped them once, and sailed into the air and in her direction. He was graceful in flight despite his enormity, and when he touched down, Qayna saw that he held a child in his arms. His son, Jacob.

Azazel set the boy down between him and Qayna, and Jacob looked up at her with bright blue eyes. This boy, tousle-headed, pale and small, but with sturdy shoulders and determination in his eyes, was his heir. His father was majestic, powerful and graceful, but Jacob looked like a mere beautiful boy. He looked as human as Qayna.

And how human was that? She thought.

For all his many women, Azazel had only managed to get one living son, and that had been done with the aid of great sorceries.

The seed of the Fallen, apparently, did not grow well in the furrows of Eve.

"You must take Jacob and flee," Azazel told her.

"The Swordbearers are here!" Qayna said, waving her weapon in a big circle to indicate that they were surrounded.

Azazel smiled gently, but there was a flash of irritation in his eyes. "Must I repeat myself?" he asked. "I took you in when you had no place else to go, Qayna. Will you not repay the favor?"

Qayna nodded heavily and grabbed Jacob by his hand.

With a heavy *CRACK!* another of the Fallen crashed to the stones behind Azazel and all three of them turned to look.

It was Semyaz. His own beast-assumed attributes included a boar's head and a long tail like a lizard's, which now flicked across the white stones of the Grand Plaza. He had wings, too, like an eagle's, feathered white and gold. The last fleeing concubines scattered, steering wide of the enormous Fallen warlord.

"Azazel!" the Fallen roared. "Your policies have failed!" With a rasp that Qayna thought must be audible outside the city, he drew a wide-bladed falchion from its scabbard at his belt and advanced on Azazel.

Suddenly, Azazel, too, was armed, his long, flaming whip appearing in his hand as if it had been there all along and Qayna had simply failed to notice it. He snapped the weapon in the space between him and the other giant, and Semyaz hesitated.

"I will happily debate the issue with you," Azazel snarled, "the next time we meet in Council!"

Semyaz straightened his back and bellowed at the trails of smoke in the sky. "I challenge you!" he roared.

Azazel cracked his whip again, but Semyaz didn't retreat. "You never had any patience for procedure, did you?" the ruler of Ainok laughed. "You can challenge me the next time the Council meets!"

Qayna dragged Jacob back, though the boy resisted. Around the edges of the Plaza, she now saw gathering others of the Fallen. They stood jittery, or they prowled with knees bent. She wondered if some of them had expected this contest.

"There is no Council, you fool!" Semyaz hissed, spraying slobber from his rubbery boar's lips. "If we do not act now, there is nothing!"

The boar-headed Fallen charged. Qayna saw the upraised scimitar and thought Azazel was doomed to die with his great city, but at the last second, the leader of the fallen cracked his whip a third time. It lashed Semyaz on his shoulder and coiled around the giant's thick, piggish neck. Then Azazel leaped aside, yanking his rival with him—

and Semyaz crashed head-first into the base of the Tower.

He sank up to his shoulders in the white stone, plowing right through a wide mirror and shattering it instantly into glass dust. The stairs above the Fallen's head shattered into gravel, and a huge crack split the rock.

"*This* to your challenge!" Azazel roared, and rammed his shoulder into Semyaz's back. He drove the other Fallen into the base of the Tower like a nail, as Semyaz squealed and wiggled but couldn't get away. More mirrors fell.

The Fallen around the Plaza hopped up and down, hissed and stared at each other. They were agitated and uncertain. Qayna pulled Jacob's hand and tried to leave down a colonnaded avenue, but a huge Fallen with a serpent's head blocked her way, tongue flicking in and out of his mouth. Qayna raised her sword, but didn't dare attack the giant creature.

"The Council is here!" boomed another of the Fallen. He was a bull-headed giant whose body was covered with scales. In his hands he hefted an enormous club, like the trunk of an entire tree with twisted metal spikes shoved entirely through it. "Semyaz has made a motion, we must vote!"

Others of the Fallen stepped forward, and Qayna jogged out of the way with the child. The serpent-headed giant kept his beady eye on her, though, and she was careful not to give the appearance of fleeing.

Around them on all sides, at the edges of the city of Ainok, smoke and fire rose in sheets. The Swordbearers were setting about their work of destruction.

Qayna's crow circled the Tower, wings stiff.

Azazel stepped into the center of the Council, whip trailing behind him on the stones. He smiled, and Qayna was reminded how majestic he was—how powerful and moving they all were, setting aside the part-animal forms. They weren't beautiful, but something in them stirred her soul.

"I apologize, Semyaz," he purred. "I didn't hear your motion. Could you repeat it for me?"

The Fallen Semyaz kicked his legs and *murmmphed*, his head still stuck in the base of the Tower. The crack split wider and crawled further up the stone.

"Semyaz questioned your policies," Bull Head growled. "He's not the only one of us who thinks you've been too soft on Eden."

Azazel arched his eyebrows and nodded slightly. "What Semyaz did," he said slowly, "was issue a challenge." He looked around at the other members of the Council. "Does anyone else here … wish to issue me … a similar challenge?"

There was a heavy silence. The ring of fire surrounding the city of Ainok was through its gates, Qayna thought, and burnings its way closer. She could hear screams, far outside the Plaza, and smell scorched flesh.

"I thought not."

Azazel turned in a flash and kicked his goat-like hoof into the posterior of his rival. Semyaz bellowed in anger, the sound muffled by the stone around his head, and was pounded deeper into the rock.

Semyaz could stand the blow, but the Tower couldn't. The widening crack became a fissure, and suddenly Qayna could see daylight through the middle of the Tower. She dragged Jacob back and away at a sprint, and this time Snake Face was too busy watching out for his own skin to get in the way.

CRASH!!!

Great blocks of masonry rained down around the Grand Plaza, crashing to the ground like falling stars and smashing up the smooth white stone. Mirrors exploded into fragments and dust, forever shattering the gates they contained. Azazel stood still, eyes flashing at his rivals as they cowered in the tumult.

Qayna managed to get behind Snake Face and then several more of the Fallen, and their bodies intercepted big chunks of rock that would have flattened her and the boy. Glass shards and gravel shrapnel still tore their skin and stung them from head to toe.

Then the Tower was flat and a cloud of white dust slowly settled over them all. Several of the Fallen lay bruised and bleeding in the wreckage, but Azazel stood tall in the center. With a single flap of his wings, he snapped the dust off his own person and the ground beneath him.

"Look at that," the founder of the city of Ainok said, glancing down at his own hoof. "You've made me split a nail."

Bull Head sneezed dust and mucus onto the stone and shook his shoulders. "The city is taken, Azazel," he rumbled, staring at his leader with yellow eyes and lowering his club. "We must do something."

"I will." Azazel dropped his whip. "I will do it now. And what you should do … all of you …" he didn't look at Qayna, but she realized he was talking particularly to her, hidden as she now was back among the ranks of the Fallen, "is flee."

Azazel, leader of the Fallen, turned and walked through the rubble of his Tower toward the main avenue of the city. In passing, he took the opportunity to kick Semyaz once more, in the belly. Semyaz grunted.

"Do not forget this day," Azazel intoned deeply. "I am yet your leader."

Qayna squeezed Jacob's hand tighter and slipped away. The Fallen around her let her go, probably didn't even notice that she was there. They hesitated only a moment, and then they turned and ran like she did, loping and scurrying and stampeding for the walls.

She didn't mean to, but Qayna found herself following a path parallel to Azazel's. She tried to turn left and move perpendicular to him, expecting that his course would take him into the heart of the action and the danger. Her way was blocked almost immediately, though; at the end of a short alley, she ran into one of the Sword-bearers.

He was a giant, as they all were, and he wore the eyeless, visorless helmet of his office. He was wingless, because the Bearers of the Sword didn't fly, they merely fell to earth to wreak their devastation. Flame erupted about the Swordbearer in a column, fire dripped like burning oil from his arms and sheets of flame trailed behind his enormous weapon. He swung his sword left and right, not like the blinded creature he appeared to be, but as if responding to some inner dictate that had nothing to do with the inputs of his senses. The weapon must be twelve feet long, Qayna thought—she had heard many stories of the Bearers of the Sword in her youth, told by the Bearers of the Word and repeated by her parents, but she had never before seen one and she felt awed. The weapon shattered wood and stone with equal facility, leaving smoking and shattered ruins behind with each blow.

One of the Fallen rushed to get past the Swordbearer, crab-like lower body scuttling with all its power and humanoid arms raising a shield and spear defensively. The Swordbearer's back-handed swing sliced through shield and spear alike, melted the crab carapace merely by passing close to it, and chopped entirely through the Fallen's torso. The Fallen burst into flame and collapsed.

The Bearer of the Sword stepped over the smoking body and moved in Qayna's direction, weapon raised.

Qayna ran. Around another corner, she found herself on the tiled edge of a canal. To one side, the collapsed rubble of several buildings blocked her way, so she yanked Jacob's hand and rushed in the other direction, her eternal crow flapping at her shoulder.

Ahead of her, and on the other side of the canal, she saw Azazel walking forward, his back turned to her. She wondered what he was doing, and so did the boy.

"Papa," he said, and pointed.

"Yes," Qayna agreed, and dragged him faster.

Azazel stopped in a broad square, surrounded not by his Fallen compatriots now but by four of the Swordbearers. He stood upon the trampled bodied of dead men and women and Fallen alike, in a sea of blood, with his city burning around him. The Bearers raised their flaming swords.

"Stop!" Azazel thundered, and the Swordbearers hesitated. "Where is your leader?"

There was no answer from the blind swordsmen of Heaven, but they didn't attack, either.

"Raphael!" Azazel yelled. "Where is the sniveling rat?"

"I'm here, traitor!" Raphael stepped into view among the smoking buildings, and his beauty took Qayna's breath away. It had been years since she had seen one of the Messengers, Bearers of the Word, and she had forgotten how stunning they were. The Fallen retained majesty and some of their beauty, but the tinkering they had done with their own forms marred them.

Raphael flapped his six wings and drifted forward.

Though the Bearer was the more beautiful of the two gigantic figures facing off, Qayna preferred the leader of the Fallen. The mere sight of Raphael, even after so much time, made her skin burn. She felt she was being punched to the ground again to have her sins tattooed upon the scroll of her body.

She shuddered and looked away.

Ahead of her, the way was blocked by a mob of people. Not fleeing citizens of Ainok, but men with swords and spears, coming her direction. Perhaps, she thought, she could bluff her way past them. "I may pretend you are my prisoner, boy," she whispered to Jacob. "Don't be frightened."

The boy nodded.

"Have you come to spout more defiance?" Raphael demanded.

Qayna tried not to be distracted and kept marching along the canal.

"What defiance?" Azazel raised his empty palms in a shrug. "I am defeated, and I have come for punishment. Only leave the others be. They harm no one. They only wish to be free."

Qayna knew that the leader of the Fallen couldn't possibly care very much about whether Semyaz or Bull Head or Snake Face were hurt by the champions of Heaven. He was more than willing to hurt them himself, brutally, in struggles for the leadership of Ainok and its people. What he must care about, she realized, was his son. He couldn't entrust the boy to any of his rivals, so he had given him instead into Qayna's care. He had given Qayna a place and people when her own had thrown her out, and now he counted on her to pay the debt.

Qayna gritted her teeth and ran faster.

She ignored the scene of the surrender across from her. One of the Swordbearers stood on the other side of the canal now, so there was no way she could cross it. To her left was a high wall with no entrance, other than the few unshattered mirrors that still hung on it, and they were no gate to Qayna. Her only way out was through a wall of armed and armored men, faces grim behind metal helmets.

She dragged Jacob towards them, yanking his arm to look fierce and pointing her dagger at him. Ainok had been her only place of refuge, and she owed it to Ainok's founder to try to save his son, if she could.

"I've seized this boy prisoner," she bluffed. "Where do I take him?"

Swords and spears bristled in her direction. The men's armor was bronze and covered in swirling letters not too dissimilar to her own tattoos. Horsehair brushes rose from their helmets, and they wore white, hip-length capes. Qayna stopped, trying to keep the grim, confident look on her face.

The leader of the armed men only stared.

"Well?" Qayna demanded, shaking Jacob by the shoulder. "I think he's someone important."

"Do you think we don't recognized the Marked Woman when we see her?" the leader asked. His voice sounded familiar and he poked his sword at her in a very unsubtle and threatening gesture. "Do you think all the sons and daughters of Adam don't know to recognize the Marked Woman on sight?"

Qayna held her position, mind racing. "Do you mistake me for one of the Fallen?" she snarled.

Out of the corner of her eye, she saw Raphael and other Messengers wrapping enormous chains around Azazel, who knelt in the square alone with his head bowed. The Swordbearers stood motionless and alert around him.

The leader of the soldiers sheathed his sword and wormed the helmet off his face. "Do you think I would not recognize my own sister?" he asked.

It was Shet. Older, bearded, a man now, but unmistakably her brother. His face was cold and bitter.

"Shet …" she whispered.

"Take them both," Shet muttered to his men, and stepped aside. "Kill the boy."

Qayna dove into the water, dragging Jacob with her.

Immediately, she clamped her mouth over the boy's and breathed the air from her lungs into his. She knew from experience that drowning wouldn't kill her, any more than fire would, or falls, or bleeding.

She had tried them all.

Jacob kicked, but she wouldn't let him go. She dropped the sword. The bottom of the canal was thick with weed and heavy garbage and she kept to it, kicking down with her legs and pulling herself along with her free hand.

Spears stabbed into the water, and arrows, but they missed. Twice, the flaming swords of the Bearers scorched through the canal about her, making the water bubble with heat and the sudden inrushing of air, but the Bearers missed her, too, and Qayna kept swimming. Jacob bit her hand, and still she wouldn't let him go.

Qayna's lungs burned, but she ignored them, knowing that she could not die. She was under the city wall, still kicking, when the weapons of her enemies disappeared and she finally felt she and the child had come to safety. Arms and legs exhausted, skin scratched and chilled, feet hammered from running across the stone, she dragged Jacob from the river outside Ainok's burning walls. In a small grove of gnarled trees, she threw him into the grass and finally sucked air into her lungs, coughing out the water she had inhaled during the long submersion.

She slapped Jacob on the chest in camaraderie, sloshing water from both their bodies. "Well, boy," she laughed. "We made it."

He didn't answer.

And then she realized that the child beside her in the trees was still and cold.

She was still pounding on his chest and trying to force air from her lungs into his when the first chunks of Ainok's masonry, charred and burning, tore from the earth and rose into a heaven thick with smoke.

CHAPTER SEVEN

FHOOM!

Jane lit the rag-and-stone missile in her hand and it erupted into a fireball. She ignored the pain. In that instant, her wards of dissembling became inadequate, and all five rock and rollers saw her.

"*Carajo!*"

Jane whistled sharply. The Mare leaped away from the tractor in her direction, and she threw the stone.

Bullseye.

KABOOM!

The tractor exploded. The flames and force of the explosion engulfed the crow, but Jane didn't bother hoping. The bird would emerge from the wreckage unscathed, as it always had.

She grabbed the rain-slick saddle with burned fingers and hurled herself onto the Mare's back. The Mare whinnied and Jane drew the Calamity Horn.

The men on the ground rolled to their knees and tried to recover dropped weapons, but the fairy dropped at her from above, shrieking a falcon war cry.

Jane aimed high and fired, *bang! bang!* forcing the falcon to drop lower—

and then urged her mount forward with her knees—

the Thracian Mare bit at the fairy with sharp teeth, chomping wing and tail and scattering a bright spray of red blood.

Twitch hit the dirt hard, in female shape, shrieking and clutching her hip.

The Mare reared up, aiming to plunge down upon the fey drummer and shatter her with implacable hooves, but Jane pulled the animal's reins and turned her back into the sorghum furrows, galloping fast. There was no particular reason to save the fairy, but neither was there any time to waste. In a wide circle around her, beyond the planted fields and the meat packing plants and the highway, she saw the burning white columns that could mean only one thing: the Bearers of the Sword had come to Dodge City.

And that was profoundly wrong.

Raphael was absent without leave. Heaven had sent her after the renegade. They had not sent their own minions, the Legate had said, because it was a case for discretion, which had made sense. If the Bearers of the Word were again disobeying orders and making decisions for themselves, Heaven would be seen as weak, as disunified. What believer could trust in a fragmented Heaven?

So why send the Swordbearers now? Had Jane failed?

Or had the Legate lied to her?

All of Jane's instincts screamed at her to *run*, and she did. She spurred the Mare into the performance of its long and turbulent life, racing for the highway, where she planned to turn and head for Oklahoma, back the way the rock and roll band and come and the opposite direction from wherever it was they were going. She wanted, as they said in the old movies, to *get the hell out of Dodge*.

But as she raced for the strip of asphalt at the end of the field, the Bearers of the Sword raced for it, too. Ahead of her, two of the fiery giants emerged from charred and smoking sorghum stalks, swords raised and ready, masked faces unreadable.

They were after her.

A law enforcement vehicle of some sort—Jane couldn't see the writing, but she saw the flashing lights on the rooftop and heard the siren—pulled to a screeching halt before the Swordbearers and two officers jumped out. As Jane veered to race back into the sorghum, she saw one of the Bearers slam his blade down like a drill, through the center of the police car's roof. The flashing lights, the roof and the entire car disappeared in a column of bright, oily flame, and the two cops scattered left and right.

Then Jane's back was turned and she lost sight of them. "Faster, girl!" she urged the Mare, and pointed her nose through the wind and the rain in the direction of the meat packing plant. This wasn't a problem, she thought. She might lose the Mare, which was a shame, but she had an easy escape route and she wouldn't look back.

Part of her wanted to turn and stand. Not fight, just stand still, in the hopes that the Swordbearers could accomplish with their titanic flaming weapons what she herself had been unable to achieve with blade, bullet, drowning, suffocation, fire, poison, curse, acid, falling, or any other of her uncounted attempts. Maybe the Bearers of the Sword could kill her.

But she didn't trust Heaven to be that merciful. If they'd wanted her dead, the Legate could simply have given her the death letter in the Las Vegas hotel room. They could have revoked the curse, or never have cursed her in the first place. Her original punishment could have been merciful execution, instead of condemnation to an eternal pilgrimage with no destination and no reward for piety.

No, Heaven wanted something, and they weren't going to ask nicely.

Racing across the furrows towards the plant, Jane tracked several things. She noticed the cordon of the Bearers of the Sword closing in. She saw the two policemen, puffing along the highway in the direction of the plant, one of them occasionally turning to fire at the flaming angels of punishment. She spotted a scarlet sedan chair approaching at a quick shuffle-step pace from the opposite direction. All of them converged on Fine Cuts, Inc.

Also closing in on the packing plant, juddering across the furrows like a spoon over a washboard, came something that almost made Jane smile: a rusted, dented, cracked, scratched and beat-to-hell brown Dodge van. Not that they were her friends; in fact, they were after her. But she admired scrappiness, and she felt akin to the down-at-the-heels, held-together-by-duct-tape-and-spit rock band. They were wanderers, outlaws and loners, just like she was. Just like she had always been.

Also, Jim was Azazel's son.

Jane considered jumping off the Mare and escaping right in the middle of the field. She'd have done it, except that she wasn't sure she had the strength. The burning fire of her ka was measured by art and intuition, and not by metric science. She knew she was recovering her strength, she thought she probably had the power to pull off now what she had planned, but she couldn't be sure.

And failure would mean capture.

Jane leaped the Mare effortlessly over the rail fence just as the sedan chair from one end and the cops from the other stumbled up to the plant. One of the officers looked panicked and out of his mind; the other was surprisingly calm, holding his fire with his pistol in its holster. She couldn't see the sedan chair's occupant through the hanging red curtains, but it was such a silly and medieval affectation that it just had to belong to the Legate. It was carried, two in front and two behind, by men who were too large, muscular and blank-stared to be normal humans. Golems, she thought. Or professional wrestlers. Given the kilts they were wearing, most likely the former.

The Bearers of the Sword were further away. They swung their swords like harvesting sickles, burning the sorghum to the ground and incinerating trees, buildings, and anything else in their way.

Behind Jane, a *crash!* told her that the brown Dodge van had smashed through the rail fence.

The potholes were full of rainwater now, end even more treacherous. A lesser animal might have broken its ankle; the Thracian Mare charged over and through the hazards without complaint.

She urged the Mare up the concrete steps on the back side of the plant and ducked, holding on to her hat. The mighty beast rushed through the back door in a single kick of its hind legs, scattering papers, jackets and rubber gloves left and right as it breezed through the entry and into the cold room.

Jane pulled the reins and the Thracian Mare skidded to a slow stop, hooves clattering across concrete. Jane tumbled off the horse, grabbing her saddlebags and slinging them over her own shoulder. She made extra sure she had the hoof fragment, tucked into her duster pocket. She wanted out, and she wasn't sure she wanted to go after the rogue Bearer of the Word anymore, not right now, but if others wanted the hoof, then it might become a valuable bargaining chip.

"Thanks, girl," she patted the horse on the rump, and then whistled the command most welcome to her mount. "Give 'em hell."

The Mare snorted jets of steam in the crisp cold of the plant, bared cat-like teeth and galloped for the back door.

"*Chingón!*"

Sudden gunfire filled the meat packing plant. The metal walls made the plant a natural reverb unit and the raucous explosions banged back and forth infinitely. The Mare took hits but didn't slow her charge, and then the entry room collapsed into total chaos, a storm of kicking hooves, chomping teeth, and flying lead.

Jane considered the bathroom doors and almost went inside, but decided against it at the last moment. If she was wrong and her ka failed her, she didn't want to be trapped in a dead end, not by the scruffy rock and rollers any more than she wanted to be trapped by the police or the Legate and his Swordbearers.

And where was Raphael in all this, after all?

Instead, she headed for the stairs, swallowing against the deafening racket of the gunfire.

As she kicked open the door she looked back and saw that she was followed. It was the singer, Jim. He ran with a bloody saber bared in his fist, crashing between the swinging beef carcasses like a freight train rushing along its cleared track through the trees of the forest, knuckles swinging and breath blasting in his nostrils.

She slammed the door in his face and raced up the stairs.

Oh, for more ka, she thought, or more time. But she'd rather be caught by the handsome singer than by the Legate—it was hard to imagine that he could do very much to her, other than cut her or inflict some transient physical pain. Heaven, on the other hand, could really hurt her. She knew that because it had.

His boots crashed into the stairwell behind her as she reached the door at the top.

She hesitated a moment, wondering if she would open the door to find a flaming sword thrust into her face. It probably wouldn't kill her, but it would hurt.

She forced herself to throw open the door and charged out onto the rooftop.

It might as well have been noon, the sky was so bright. Directly overhead, in a tiny circle, she could still see stars. They twinkled like will o' the wisps at the bottom of a deep, black well. A circle of white light blanched out the host of heaven around that bottomless well, and then streaked and blurred, in some places almost imperceptibly, into a ring of fire giants standing still and ready around the plant. There were seven of them, and they stood with swords help upright, fire dripping down to further scorch the ruined fields and mar the asphalt and gravel. The furnace blaze of their fire dried the air up, so that the wind gusting across the rooftop was arid and no rain fell.

Jane cursed, the Adamic imprecation blowing a small crater in the gravel at her feet.

She slammed the door shut behind her, wishing she could know exactly how much ka she had, so that she could throw a ward of sealing onto the exit. It didn't matter, she was almost gone, anyway. She couldn't see the sedan chair or the policemen from where she was, only the implacable giants, faces visored shut and angelic bodies still and ready to pounce.

She heard gunshots, though. Lots of gunshots, and the fierce, blood-drinking whinny of the Thracian Mare.

She raced to the circle she had left on the lightning-bolt-bearing box; it was intact. Jane dropped her saddlebags to the rooftop and clambered atop the metal casing. The circle was not exactly the one she would have preferred, either to regenerate the heat of her ka or to strengthen her gate-opening incantation. Its glyphs were written in Adamic, though, which gave it power and would reinforce her in anything she did; it would have to suffice.

Jane pulled a small round mirror from the saddlebag and set it on the metal at her feet without looking at it. She kept her eyes on the burning giants, ready to leap into action if they tried anything. She had the Calamity Horn, after all; one bullet per Swordbearer was terrible odds and a gamble, but at least she could make them think twice about trying to take her against her will.

She heard the rooftop door smash open, and she turned to face Jim, the singer. He came rushing across the gravel with his sword in hand, but he didn't move like a fencer, cautious, one foot in front of the other. He sprinted, head down and glaring like a bull.

Jane incanted the words in Adamic and felt the fire of her ka flow from her. She waved good-bye at the charging rock and roller, smiled, and stepped onto the mirror—

nothing happened.

She looked down, and saw that the reflective glass had gone dull and gray. Jane cursed again, not meaning to, and the glass cracked.

Jim stabbed at her—

Jane stepped sideways, but a little too late. The burning in her side where his saber cut into her flesh jerked her back to full wakefulness and attention, and Jane dropped backwards off the generator box, drawing her knives.

Jim stabbed again, and a third time, but the box was in the way. He stepped forward and executed a neat shoulder roll across the top of the metal—

Jane stepped in slashing, but was forced back by the heavy heels of his boots before she could land a good blow, and then he pressed her again.

Something bowled into the small of Jane's back, knocking her forward. Frantically, she crossed her long knife blades in front of her and caught Jim's saber blade in them. She pushed, trying to shove the blade out of the way—

and instead, she impaled herself on it. The sword sank into her belly, up to the hilt.

Jane fell heavily, dragging Jim's weapon with her. With confused vision, she saw a white horse flashing red, and for a moment she imagined that the Thracian Mare was coming to her rescue, but then she remembered that the Mare was black, and she realized that the horse she was seeing was the fairy Twitch; that the flashes of red were Twitch's blood where Jane herself had caused injury.

Then Twitch the horse kicked Jane in her head, throwing her body sideways and slamming her to the roof again.

Jane tried to think as she dragged herself away. The band wanted Azazel's hoof back. Did Heaven want the hoof as well, was that what this was about? The angel caretaker of Dudael had failed, and Jane had been sent to recover what had been stolen?

But then why not tell her as much?

"Stop," she croaked. Twitch kicked her again, still in horse form, and smashed her flat to the gravel. "I'm not sure we're enemies." She dribbled the words from her lips with a thin stream of blood.

Jim lifted her off the ground far enough to grab the hoof clipping in her pocket and extract it in a single tug.

"You can't trust her, Jim," the fairy said, and Jane saw her leather boots, with neat rows of shiny metal spikes running up past the ankle on the outside of each boot. *Crack!* She punched Jane in the back of her head with one of her wooden batons.

Ouch. Jane needed to stop getting hit. She raised one arm, and when the fairy's next blow came down, she caught it on the flesh of her forearm and managed to wrap her fingers around the wood.

"Stop," she ground out through the hot blood in her mouth.

She heard an animal scream, and guessed it was the Mare. She felt surprisingly bad for having led the beast to its death. She'd killed and betrayed so many of her own kind, it struck her as incongruous that she should feel like shedding tears for a flesh-eating horse.

She rolled away on her shoulder, dragging the long steel blade with her free hand until it fell out of her body with a wet *pop*.

Jim stood to one side. He held the hoof and looked vaguely puzzled.

"Oberon's tail," Twitch gasped, staring at Jane and stepping back. "You hear a thing a thousand times, but you don't believe it until you see it."

Jane spat blood onto the muddy gravel and lay back. She couldn't breathe now; felt like she was drowning and she was sure it was blood in one of her lungs. It didn't matter. She knew it wouldn't kill her, and in a few moments, the pain would pass. She spat out blood again. "Oberon doesn't have a tail."

Twitch snorted. "And God doesn't have teeth, but that didn't keep anyone from swearing by them for a thousand years, did it?"

Jim bent and slowly picked up his sword. He looked around.

Jane sat up. The Swordbearers loomed large and not far away. A collective step forward, Jane thought, and they could bring their swords down together and reduce the meat packing plant to charred brick and burned ribs. Why weren't they attacking?

And what had happened to her mirror?

And what was really going on here?

"How do you know God doesn't have teeth?" she asked.

"Ah," the fairy sighed, "how do you think? Hadn't you heard he was one of us?"

Jane dragged herself to her feet. The blood had stopped gushing down her chest, but she felt weak and her ka was all but gone, a dim pulsing within her barely worthy of the name. "If God really is one of the folk of the Mirror Queendom," she cracked, "that would explain why Heaven always seems to get everything backward."

"Sir?" a voice elsewhere on the rooftop called. "Sir, this is a … this is a crime scene, and I have to ask you to leave."

Jane turned and saw the Legate, in his mantelletta and galero, stomping her direction across the rooftop. Behind him came two of his big sedan slaves, and now Jane saw that they were indeed golems; they breathed heavy, with their mouths open, and she could see the Hebrew characters tattooed on their tongues.

After the Legate came two law enforcement officers, Sheriff's deputies, Jane now saw. The younger man, with buzzcut hair and a thin mustache, walked in front. He called out to the Legate, asking the red-caped man to stop and getting a cold shoulder in return. Behind him came an older, heavier deputy, with a beard and a paunch and his hand resting on the butt of a gun at his hip.

"And you there," Mustache continued, pointing at Jim. His finger trembled. "Drop your sword, sir, so we can have a polite conversation about what's going on here." The deputy looked around at the Bearers of the Sword that surrounded the building. "A polite conversation that also made some damn kinda sense would be a nice bonus."

Jim tightened his grip on his sword, but frowned like he didn't understand the Deputy's words. Jane was sure she had seen him somewhere before, though not recently.

"Thank you, Qayna," the Legate said. He stopped and sat on the metal casing of the generator. "You've done exactly as we'd hoped."

"Funny," Jane bluffed. "So have you. It's over."

"Everyone here should consider himself under arrest!" Deputy Mustache insisted, pointing his pistol at the ground beside the

Legate. "You with the sword, put it down ... now!"

"Raphael," the Legate said, and his voice sounded old. "Can we end this?" The golems lurked behind him like exclamations marks waiting to jump onto all of his sentences.

Deputy Beard drew his pistol, a large-caliber revolver. "You heard the man." He raised the gun.

"Thanks, pard," Deputy Mustache glared at Jim.

"It's over," Beard said.

Bang!

Deputy Mustache fell to the ground, bleeding from the back of his head.

"Thank you, Rafi," the Legate said. "Now, let's get down to a little business, shall we?" He removed from under his mantelletta a familiar piece of sealed and folded parchment, and waved it until it caught Jane's attention.

Raphael and the Legate were in cahoots, Jane realized.

She'd been set up.

CHAPTER EIGHT

here never was any renegade," Jane said calmly. The mirror gate must not have worked because the Legate, or someone working with him, had pinned it shut. She looked at Jim, blinking and shaking his head like he had water in his ears, and wondered if the Legate had done something to the singer, too.

"No, there wasn't," Beard agreed. He held his gun with antsy hands, and not with the sure calmness of an experienced shooter. "Or rather, there hasn't been one yet. Soon, there'll be many."

He laughed, and the Legate laughed with him.

"Jim?" Twitch asked, but got no answer.

Jane's curse-driven powers of recuperation were kicking in, and she was starting to feel stronger.

"This has all been a trap," Jane added, ruminating.

The golems growled an objection in unison.

"No," the Legate objected, showing his palms in protest and waving back his sedan team. "What trap? This has all been an invitation. We wanted to arrange a meeting of certain key people." He waved the letter again, tantalizingly. "I assure you that I have only the best of intentions."

"You wanted us to meet you under guard," Jane pointed out, nodding at the Swordbearers. "And stoned."

The Legate waved a hand and muttered something under his breath; that he was a sorcerer came as no surprise, and Jane wondered how good he was. Jim shook his head, his eyes suddenly cleared. He raised his sword an inch or two and took half a step forward, but then halted at the Legate's upraised hand.

"Please, James," the Legate said. "I had to be sure you wouldn't run. But as a sign of good faith, I've cloaked this entire building with wards of silence. Please feel free to join the conversation. I *want* to hear what you have to say."

Jim narrowed his eyes and flared his nostrils.

"Oh, you shouldn't imagine me using the unreliable, spotty, flaring wards of your erratic little wizardling," the Legate assured him. Then he laughed. "Believe me, I'm just as anxious as you are not to be heard by His Lowness at this moment. We'll talk to Lucifer when the time is right, but not before."

"Call off your dogs," Jim rumbled. His voice had something of the trumpet in it, and reminded Jane of the voices of the Fallen. The golems growled at him as if prompted, but the Swordbearers remained impassive and still.

"You must understand me clearly." The Legate's eyes were serious. "We are going to have a conversation now, and that conversation *will—absolutely* and *without question*—go the way I want it to. The Bearers are just here to see to that."

Deputy Beard holstered his pistol and sneered at Twitch. "Miaow."

Twitch hissed at him through her teeth.

Jane stared at the Deputy. His true identity—the name and nature of the being that lurked inside the Deputy's body, animating and controlling him—was still sinking into her consciousness. "Raphael," she said softly. "It has been a very long time."

"Qayna," he nodded.

"I don't usually go by that name." Jane itched all over. It felt like the ink of her tattoos crawled under her skin at the sight of the person who had first etched them into her. She spat on the gravel.

"There is war coming," the Legate intoned. "War in Heaven. Michael and his angels against the dragon."

"The Revelation of John," Jim said. "The refuge and comfort of every crackpot for the last two thousand years." Something burning behind his eyes suggested to Jane that he didn't quite believe his own words.

"War is inevitable!" Raphael shot back. "You can't build a kingdom on lies!"

Jane disagreed: "I'm not sure you can build a kingdom on anything else." She was recovering from the shock of realizing that she was again seeing Raphael, and now she felt anxious to shoot him.

If not for the fact that her own death was in play, a golden worm baiting a tiny hook, she'd have shot him already.

"Cynic!" Raphael was shocked.

Jane shrugged, not meeting the Messenger's eyes. "I've been around too long to be an idealist. What are you going on about?"

"Accept for the moment that war is coming," the Legate said. He shrugged. "Accept it because, if nothing else, I will start that conflict myself. The questions you should be asking yourselves are *what do I want out of the coming and unavoidable conflict?* And *how am I going to get it?*"

"The war between Michael and the dragon." Jim raised his eyebrows. "You're planning to invade Hell?"

"The dragon is a poetic image." The Legate folded his hands piously in his lap. "Perhaps *I* am the dragon."

"So Michael throws you to the earth," Jim followed the logic dubiously, "and you become Satan. You have strange aspirations, Legate. Even my father didn't *want* his fate."

Jane stared hard at Jim, wondering how much he knew, and wondering whether it was true that Azazel hadn't wanted his throne.

"Poetry!" the Legate hissed. He composed himself again.

"Who knew that the titles of the head of the Infernal Council were poetic?" Twitch laughed skeptically. "The Infernals, anyway, seem to take them very seriously."

"It might have been the title," Jim muttered to the fairy, "or it might have been the fart jokes."

Jane felt as nonplussed as the Legate looked.

The man in the mantelletta shook off his confusion. "Forget the Bible. Here's the point. Each of you is carrying a bargaining chip. I will not deceive you or play the coquette—I want what you have, and I will pay."

"*We* want," Raphael corrected him, but the Legate ignored the angel.

Jane looked around at the Swordbearers, gigantic and fiery, immobile in the clouds of smoke that their burning threshed out of the sorghum around their feet. "In other words," she said with deliberate impudence, "you want to kill me, and in exchange, you'll let me torture and kill Raphael first."

The Angel-Deputy chuckled, but turned a little pale. Jane stared him down with an eye full of thousands of years of constantly nurtured hatred.

The Legate fixed her with a stare. "I want the Calamity Horn," he said. "The gun capable of killing even immortals."

"Except me," Jane pointed out. "To my grave disappointment."

"Forgive the pun," the fairy snapped out reflexively.

"I never forgive puns," Jim grunted. "They remind me too much of what I'm missing by holding my tongue all the time."

The Legate smiled patiently. "So you don't need to fear handing it over. Besides, you already know that your death is within my gift." He waved the letter at her. It was so close that Jane could *smell* the parchment and the sealing wax.

Jane's crow settled beside the Legate on the metal box.

Within his gift. That sounded right; the Legate wasn't trying to kill her outright, but was offering her the chance to be able to die. He was doing more than offering—he was selling it, pretty hard.

"I don't fear much of anything at this point. Still, I'm curious." Jane squinted at the big singer. "You must be invading Hell, right? I mean, there are precious few beings this gun is capable of hurting that you couldn't just take down with the Swordbearers. But even the Fallen, they can be beaten with flaming swords." She glared at Raphael, remembering the obliteration of Ainok. "So why the gun?"

"And seven priests," the Legate said in answer, "bearing seven trumpets of rams' horns before the ark of the Lord went on continually, and blew with the trumpet."

Jane snorted. "You don't need to quote me chapter and verse on this stuff. I was there for most of it."

"There for what?" Twitch asked. "I don't know either the chapter or the verse. I'm not much of a reader."

"Joshua's priests blew seven horns and the walls of Jericho came tumbling down."

Jim looked at her with a curious smile. "What was that like?"

"I was on the wall." Jane shrugged. "It hurt like hell, but I survived."

"And I saw the seven angels which stood before God; and to them were given seven trumpets." The Legate's eyes twinkled.

"Back to Revelation? Seven priests with trumpets before the ark, seven seraphim with trumpets before the throne." Jim shrugged. "Sort of a match, I guess, but lots of things come in sevens. Seven sages of Greece. Seven colors in the visible spectrum. Snow White and the seven dwarfs. So what?"

A long spate of gunshots ended in an abrupt equine scream.

Jane frowned. "Seven bullets in my gun is so what," she realized out loud.

"The first angel sounded," Raphael quoted, "and there followed hail and fire mingled with blood, and they were cast upon the earth: and the third part of trees was burnt up, and all green grass was burnt up."

"You'd like that, wouldn't you, you son of a bitch?" Jane remembered the fields of her youth, the moist, firm feeling of earth between her fingers. She almost yanked the pistol out and started firing.

"You think the seven bullets in her gun," Jim pointed at it to underline the insanity of the idea, "are the seven trumpets of the apocalypse? This is what I'm hearing from the Legate of Heaven?"

"Ah, I hate this stuff," Twitch muttered. "Jehoshaphat begat Arad who begat Shem, gobbledy-gobbledy, can't we just skip to the part where we start shooting? Why is life on this side of the mirror always so tedious?"

"Maybe," Jim said, "just *maybe*, we can avoid the shooting this time."

"I doubt it." Jane stared hard at the angel who had tattooed her body, thousands of years ago.

"Gavrilo's Horn," the Legate said. "Don't you see?"

Raphael continued; spittle flecked his chin. "And the second angel sounded, and as it were a great mountain burning with fire was cast into the sea."

"Prophecy is prophecy." The Legate nodded. "It will be fulfilled, whatever I do. I am merely trying to discover a way to fulfill it ... advantageously."

"And the third angel sounded, and there fell a great star—"

"Shut up!" Jim snapped.

Raphael arched his eyebrows and closed his mouth.

"Bat-shit crazy." Azazel's son shook his head. "Give me one reason why I shouldn't walk away from you and your madness."

"Because I will give you what you want, James."

Jane looked into the singer's eyes and saw the truth: he was curious, and he was tempted.

At that moment the rooftop's door opened and the other rock and rollers staggered out. Eddie led the way, sawed-off shotgun in his hands, and behind him followed Mike holding a two-by-four and Adrian squinting through his sorcerer's lens.

The golems turned to look at the newcomers and raised their fists defensively, but didn't attack.

Jim raised a hand, palm out, to stop the band's advance.

"Careful!" Adrian shouted back. "There's all kinds of crazy warding and hexes on this building!"

Jim nodded slowly.

"We had this conversation before, Raphael," he said.

"No. I tried to have this conversation, and you refused."

While they were looking at each other, Jane carefully slipped the edge of her duster aside, to be sure she had a clean draw when she needed it.

"What do I want, then?" Jim asked.

"Jim, don't do it," Twitch urged his friend.

"Whatever you want," the Legate told him, "you can get it with power. Power brings all good things. Power, and money, which is the same thing."

"That's true!" Adrian called out, and Mike elbowed him in the chest.

"I could have any woman I wanted," Jim suggested.

"They'd line up." The Legate smiled a pimp's greasy grin.

"Hey!" Mike threw in. "Share!" Adrian elbowed him back.

"Wealth." Jim grinned. "The kingdoms of this world. All I have to do is bow down to you."

"All of them could be yours. And you don't have to bow down to anyone, including me. You'll never have to bow down to anyone ever again."

"I could finally afford to fix the leaky radiator on the van."

The Legate's smile became uncertain. "You could have any car you wanted."

Jim's smile disappeared into a flat, hard line. "I want the damn van."

Raphael shrugged. "So keep the van," he said.

"He's saying *no*." The Legate frowned.

Jim raised his sword and shook its basket hilt at the Legate's galero. "I'm saying you don't know me from Adam," he growled.

"Tell me what you want."

"No!" Jim snapped. Suddenly, he seemed huge, and his voice echoed over the rooftop so loud that even the Swordbearers appeared to stir a little at the sound. "You tell me what *you* want, Legate! What are you doing chasing me down in the middle of nowhere? What do you want, the hoof, is that it? All this for a toenail clipping?"

The Legate and the angel were both silent. Jim towered taller than either of them with his naked sword in his hand, threatening and dangerous.

"If it's just a toenail clipping," the Messenger said slowly, "why don't you give it up?"

Jim barked a short "ha!"

"What is Heaven?" the Legate asked.

"You're asking the wrong guy," Jim snarled. "I've never been."

"Heaven is a palace." The Legate sniffed. "It has gardens, like any palace. The air of Heaven is delicious with the tinkle of fountains and running water. It has a staff, with servants who perform different functions. Some are guards and warriors, others clerks and scribes, still others guides and major-domos."

"And presumably some gardeners," Twitch added. "Won't anybody think of the poor plants?"

The quip cut through all the tension and endeared the fairy to Jane, and she winked. Twitch arched an eyebrow back, in surprise and maybe fear.

"At the center of the palace complex is the audience chamber," the Legate continued. "Here the angels keep burning the eternal fires, maintain the perpetual cloud of incense, and so forth."

"Get to the point."

"Beyond the audience chamber lies the throne room," the Legate continued, unperturbed. "But within the throne room, and at its veil, stand the seven seraphim."

"I remember these guys," Jim agreed, and nodded in Raphael's direction. "Your boy was making fun of them, last time we met."

Raphael shrugged.

"The seven are great and terrible," the Legate went on. "One for each of the seven lights on the great golden tree, they are nameless, faceless beings of eternal fire."

"And beyond them is the throne, and on the throne sits God," Jim finished the Legate's account.

The Legate was silent.

"Did I miss a step?" Jim pressed. "Did I forget the bottle-washing angels, or the shoe polishers, or the angels who wax on and wax off?"

The Legate shook his head.

"Maybe I left out the legions of tortured sufferers," Jim suggested. "Hanging on racks in the kingdom of Heaven to suffer until Judgment Day because their mortal lives weren't suffering enough! Oh, wait, no, Heaven doesn't want *those* people ... it sends them away, to somewhere more fitting for them."

"Is that what you want?" the Legate asked slowly. "You want to free the damned souls in Hell?"

"What I *want*," Jim roared, so loud and fierce that Jane took a step back and her hand strayed close to her gun, "is to be *left alone!* By *you*, by my *father*, and by *everyone else!*"

He looked like his father in that moment, and it took Jane's breath away.

He also looked like Jacob, whom she had killed without meaning to.

"I don't care *who* sits on that throne," Jim bellowed, "so long as he leaves me in *peace!*"

"*No one* sits on the throne!" the Legate charged to his feet, veins popping out in his head.

Jim checked his tirade.

"No one?" Jane asked.

"No one." The Legate sank back to his seat.

"Who runs Heaven, then?" Twitch asked. "You can't have a kingdom without a king, can you?"

"No one," the Legate said again.

"The seraphim." Raphael said it with conviction, and liked the sound of it so much that he said it again. "The seraphim. It has to be."

"You're right, child of Mab," the Legate agreed. "A kingdom with no king is an abomination. It's a ship without a captain, and must run aground. We have to end this terrible situation."

"How do you know there's no captain at the wheel?" Twitch asked. "What did you do, sneak a peek when nobody was looking? There's not even a little man behind the curtain, pulling on levers, no one?"

The Legate ignored the questions.

"You're not going to invade *Hell*," Jane clarified. "You're going to invade *Heaven*. And you need the Calamity Horn so you can shoot the seraphim with it."

"Then why do you need me?" Jim demanded. "Take the gun. Kill her. She wants it. Look at her, you can see it in her eyes. Only leave me alone! I am not a part of your revolution, I have nothing to do with my father."

"Is that how your father sees it, too?" the Legate asked softly. "Does he have nothing to do with you?"

Jim said nothing.

"We need your father and his hordes." The Legate spoke quietly, but with a note of finality in his voice like he was pronouncing sentence.

"You have the Swordbearers," Jim said.

The Legate shook his head. "They are here to execute a Writ, and only because Qayna was good enough to put Raphael's life in danger."

"I'll be better than that," Jane muttered.

"We have sympathizers." The Legate smiled. "The third part of the host of heaven, I believe, is the traditional figure. But they won't take up arms unless they are confident of victory. We need the Horn, and we need your father's help."

"I want nothing to do with it," Jim insisted.

"If you refuse," the Legate said deliberately, "then we will have to kill you, and use your father's hoof as a lever to involve him anyway. I can't have you running around free with this knowledge, James."

"Kill me."

The Legate arched his eyebrows, nodded, and turned to Jane. "Kill him," Heaven's rebel emissary told her, "and the death letter is yours."

"Go to Hell." Jane laughed. "Pun intended." Lightning flashed across the well of darkness overhead, and the rain picked up, heavy enough now to pummel its way down through the ring of fire and splash Jane in the face.

The Legate's eyes flashed with irritation. "Raphael—" he began.

The golems stepped forward.

Jane's fingers brushed the butt of the Calamity Horn. "Go for your gun, you angelic son of a bitch." She stared at Raphael, eyes boring through the puppet-mask of the Deputy's body and imagining the six-winged Bearer of the Word within. "I'm begging you, *please*, as a personal favor to me, go for your gun."

CHAPTER NINE

Fat drops of rain spattered Qayna's face as she dropped down
from the ridge and into the open mouth of Hell.

The slope was muddy and she fell more than once on the
way down, coating her doe-skin tunic in gray slime. Her nostrils
rebelled against the stink of the crater and her eyes shied away from
the multitude of dead and dying birds that lay floating in it. Her
own crow circled above the hole in the ground, indifferent to
whatever killed all the other fliers. The mud was not the result of
the rain—it and the few scattered drops were the after-leavings, the
remnants, the stirrings in the wake of the flood.

The *Flood*, Qayna knew that Shet's descendants would forever
after call it. The windows of heaven had opened and the fountains
of the deep had ruptured and everything Qayna had ever known
had been obliterated by choppy water.

Qayna had drowned.

Only it hadn't killed her. And after several long days of painful
torture, being dragged about by the currents of the deep and
gnawed by one strange, eyeless monster after another, she had
admitted to herself that, whatever the Flood might do to the Fallen
and their children, it wasn't going to end her existence.

She'd armed herself with weapons that wouldn't weigh her
down: knives. Then she'd swum to the top, flung herself upon the

gnarled, beheaded floating trunk of a tree and begun coughing mud and brine from her lungs. She was still hacking up black ooze when Nuh's boat had passed her by, old Nuh (white bearded and bent over, though he was hundreds of years younger than Qayna—Father and Shet and everyone she had known in her youth all long dead, other than the Fallen and Raphael) oblivious to her, standing on the deck of his bowed, air-tight ship and scratching the long neck of a giraffe.

Qayna hadn't bothered to try to get his attention.

After the Flood had come the monsters. The storm and high water had wiped out the people—the many—who had loved the city of Ainok and embraced its rule, but they also guaranteed that anything that survived them, anything that didn't come off Nuh's weird floating wooden chest, would be preternaturally tough.

Things already living in the deep had survived the hammering of cold water and crawled out hungry and pissed. The ugliest, strongest, most misshapen experiments and progeny of the Fallen had also made it through forty days and nights of rain and the slow receding afterwards. Qayna had been glad to be armed—she had pricked more than one monster into leaving her alone, and used her knives to hack her way to freedom after learning that even the digestive juices of a scabrous, six-legged land whale weren't enough to free her from Heaven's curse.

Most of the Fallen had also survived. Other than Azazel, Raphael and Shet and their army hadn't taken prisoners, and once they had razed Ainok to the ground they had lost interest in pursuing the fleeing survivors. After the Flood, Qayna had more than once hidden in a mud-strangled copse or under a shattered roof or in a festering pile of dead bodies to avoid attracting the attention of one of Ainok's rebel lords.

Bull Head had nearly stepped on her.

Weeks later, the higher ground had begun to dry out—like Ararat, where Nuh and his people had settled—but most of the face of the land was still a mud flat, pocked with ruins and the few trees tenacious enough to have hung on through the devastation. And, on the trail of a rumor she found hard to believe, Qayna returned to Ainok.

To find it a gaping hole.

And at the bottom, with yellow light flickering from it, an opening.

Qayna scrambled to her feet in a thick, fetid pool at the bottom of the crater. This might be exactly the spot where the Grand Plaza of Ainok had once been, she thought, though it was hard to be sure with most of the local landmarks obliterated. As if to confirm her guess, she stubbed her toe on a block of white stone the size of her torso.

"Password?" The voice was slithery-huge, a serpent's hiss, and Qayna recognized the snake-headed giant who had hemmed her and Jacob in when she had tried to escape the Plaza before. He wore a kilt and sandals and stood in front of a cavern entrance vast enough to hold a small town, smoke and light and movement enlivening the space behind him vaguely. She chuckled. It pleased her sense of irony that this same Fallen who had tried to keep her trapped would now try to keep her out.

"It isn't funny," Snake Face protested. "Tell me the password, or I'll kill you."

"I don't have a password," Qayna said. "But I'd like to be polite about this. How about you let me in because I'm an old friend of Azazel's? Or at least, could you tell him Qayna is here? I used to come in and out of Ainok freely."

"Those were more trusting times." The Fallen snatched her from the mud with both hands and sank his long fangs into her belly and chest. Qayna quivered and jerked, but tried not to react, letting the long saber-like teeth completely impale her. She burned as her veins filled with venom, and her limbs shook.

Then the giant threw her to the mud. She hit with a loud *splat!* and bounced. There she lay still a moment, letting the fire raging in her veins cool a bit.

"Fool," the serpent-headed colossus hissed, and resumed his station in front of the cave mouth.

Qayna climbed to her feet. "That's just what I was going to say." The Fallen gaped.

"You could bite me again," Qayna said. "It would hurt me again. But it still wouldn't kill me." She drew her longest knife and held it ready. "And this time, I'll stab you back, right in the soft tissues inside your mouth."

Snake Face hissed in irritation, but he snapped his mouth shut and he stepped aside. The crow led the way.

The mephitic stink of the crater was even thicker inside the cave. Qayna's lungs ached, but it was less painful than being buried under the Flood.

The vastness of the cavern shrank but it never became less than huge, a rough-hewn, rock-ribbed tunnel descending at a steep angle into the bowels of the earth. It never fully dried out, either, though the air became warm and the moisture consolidated into a reddish trickle of a stream in one corner of the passage, leaving crunchy footing on the rest of the floor. Light came from sputtering red torches set irregularly into brackets in the wall.

At least the dead birds were gone.

Qayna walked forever. When she had finished walking, there was a gate. Beside it waited a giant figure in breastplate, greaves and kilt, leaning on a spear. He looked totally human, other than the scabby bird-like talons that jutted into the gravelly earth under his greaves. Under long, white hair, his face was mostly grave, with just a tiny hint of a smile playing around his lips.

"Again?" she asked.

The giant shook his head. "I am Baraqyel," he said. "I'm not going to bite you."

"Stabbing me with a spear won't work, either. Trust me."

Baraqyel ignored the joke and turned away. "I am to bring you to the meeting of the Council."

Qayna followed him, through the enormous doors, which opened at his slightest touch. "Does that mean it's true?" she asked. "Azazel has returned, and is once again Head of the Council?"

"Azazel has returned," Baraqyel agreed. "Whether he is to preside is the issue that is now before the Princes."

Beyond the gates, chaos reigned. Gibbering, moaning howls filled Qayna's ears, and her eyes were unwillingly stuffed full of the spectacle of torture. A mob of people—humans, people of her stature—ravened and tore at each other, impaled each other on spikes, pummeled and clawed at each other's faces and tore each other limb from limb.

She felt sick.

With his spear, Baraqyel carved a path through the bodies. As she walked among them, Qayna looked into the eyes of the writhing tortured torturers and saw bottomless need and black despair.

"What's wrong with them?" Qayna asked her guide.

"They are dead," he told her, "and unhappy."

Qayna looked over her shoulder as she followed Baraqyel out of the cavern and up a spiral stair on the other side. Maybe, she thought, she shouldn't be so eager for her own death.

Another long corridor, full of arches and grated windows, erupted at its end out of the rough face of a jagged stone wall, and became an arching bridge. Over her shoulder, she saw that the wall both dropped and climbed out of sight, apparently infinite.

Qayna followed Baraqyel out along the slender catwalk until it terminated in another door, this one in the side of a ponderous, impossibly huge stalactite. Creatures guarded the door, hunch-backed, slithering things whose claws scratched on the stone and whose long tongues waggled suggestively at Qayna.

Her guide battered them aside with the butt of his spear. "Wait here," he instructed Qayna, and then he entered the door, shutting it behind him and leaving her alone with the creatures.

One ogled her with mismatched eyes, one enormous and the dark yellow color of a sick man's urine and the other wide and almond-shaped, with a green pupil like a cat's. The other rubbed four filthy, long-nailed hands together, scratching at its own bleeding knuckles and snickering.

"I bite," she warned them, and spat on the floor.

The door opened again and Baraqyel whisked her inside. "Keep quiet."

The interior of the stalactite was a single room dominated by a circular table, its surface above Qayna's head. One seat at the table was larger than the others, a throne, and the space before it was slightly raised. It was vacant. The other seats were filled with the princes of the Fallen, most of whom Qayna knew by sight only. There was tusked Semyaz, there was Bull Head, there was Ezeq'el the centauress. Their faces, where Qayna's view wasn't blocked by her poor angle, wore expressions of fear, surprise, disgruntlement, confusion, anger, malice, greed, and fatigue.

Azazel sat among them and smiled.

"Again I object." Semyaz glared at her with his piggish eyes and flapped his eagle's wings once.

"You object for the wrong reasons," Bull Head rumbled. "Don't object just because Azazel made a motion."

"Is no one allowed to object to anything Azazel says?" Semyaz snorted pig slobber onto his own chest and the table. "Has he become our lord and master without discussion?"

Bull Head stomped to his feet and pounded the table with his knuckles. "You waste my time, Semyaz! And you look like a petulant child!"

"Enough!" Azazel shouted.

Bull Head opened his mouth to say something and Azazel cut him off with a flick of his hand.

"Enough, Yamayol."

Bull Head nodded slightly and dropped himself back into his seat.

"She has no right," Semyaz sulked.

"She is the Marked Woman." Azazel slowly stood. "She was present at the beginning, and I think she will be present at the end. She has every right. She is the witness. Besides," he smiled again, and Qayna almost felt charmed by the titanic bat-winged and goat-legged Fallen, "we have already voted on this point of order, Semyaz, and you have lost."

Baraqyel shepherded Qayna into a corner. There was nothing in the room but the table and its seats, so Qayna assumed she was condemned to *witness* from an impossibly bad vantage point, but Baraqyel stooped without a word, lifted her and placed her on his shoulder. His white hair covered her legs like a cloak.

"I call for the question," Ezeq'el announced. With her horse's body, she stood beside the table rather than sitting in a chair. "Enough yammering. Our situation is clear, our choices are simple."

"Second," Bull Head lowed.

"The question has been called for," Azazel said. "All in favor."

A ragged unanimity of hands approved the motion.

"The candidates for President of the Infernal Council," the bat-winged Fallen continued, "bearing the titles Lucifer, Satan, the Adversary, Moloch, the King of Hell, are Semyaz ..." the boar-headed giant grunted and raised a hand in acknowledgement, "Belial …" a mass of tentacles and scaly flanks at the far end of the table shuddered, "and Azazel … that's me.

"All in favor of Semyaz … Belial … Azazel."

Hands rose in three waves, Baraqyel voting for Azazel along with many others, and then Semyaz jumped to his feet bellowing. "A tie! Deadlock! No ruler, or a triumvirate!"

"Vote again!" "Kill one of them!" "No!" An explosion of animal noises and yelling dominated the chamber for long moments.

"Silence!" Azazel roared one word, and the racket cut off. He looked across the Council chamber at Qayna. "Do you abstain, then?" he asked her.

Qayna almost fell from her perch. Her crow settled slowly on the back of the empty throne and stared at her. "Me?"

"It's a trick!" Semyaz howled, and his supporters pounded on the table with their fists and stamped on the floor with their hooves. "He's cheating!"

"Point of order!" Belial shrieked. The voice from the mass of tentacles sounded like metal grinding on metal, but somehow it formed intelligible words. "All parties present vote." Something like a beak, beneath something like a golden eye, shoved its way forward through the tentacles and fixated on Qayna. "He has done you hurt, woman. I have not."

"All parties present vote," Bull Head agreed.

"No!"

"She is the Marked Woman," Azazel repeated. "She's practically one of us."

"All parties present vote," Ezeq'el agreed.

They all stared at Qayna. She stared back, wondering whom she would offend if she said anything. She didn't mind the thought of being killed, but she balked at the idea of being trapped in the torture-orgy below.

"No!" the boar-headed Fallen Prince roared, and his hand fell to the hilt of the falchion at his belt.

The table froze. Somewhere under the table, a claw scratched nervously on stone.

"Do you challenge?" Ezeq'el drawled slowly.

Semyaz's eyes flitted around the table, counting his friends and enemies.

"No," Yamayol rumbled.

For a long moment, Jane wasn't sure Semyaz agreed.

Then Semyaz took his hand away from his weapon. "Call for a new vote!" he growled, banging the table again. "New vote!"

"Point of order," Ezeq'el said calmly. "This vote isn't over until all participants have indicated their vote."

"New vote!"

"Point of order!"

Azazel smiled.

Ezeq'el, the centauress, fixed Qayna squarely in the eye and arched one eyebrow.

"Put me down," Qayna said, and Baraqyel did so.

Some of the Fallen stared at her, but most of them stamped, bellowed and shrieked at each other.

"But ... the vote," Baraqyel said gently.

"Yes," she agreed. "The vote."

And then she turned and left the room.

She crossed the bridge at a brisk walk, forged her way through the passages and found herself standing over the field of mutually-abusive dead, staring at their pain and wondering what she had done, and why something seemed to be missing.

Then Azazel joined her, calm and quiet, with her crow on his shoulder.

That was it, she thought. For one brief moment, the crow hadn't followed her.

"You tried to use me," she accused him. She couldn't look at him, just smelled the goatness of his presence by her side. "That was unkind."

"Was it?"

There was a pause, but any silence there might have been was shattered by the shrieks of the sufferers below.

"Did you win?"

"The vote is suspended." Azazel laughed. "Semyaz and his friends are poring over the rules looking for a way out. You've set us back quite a bit—I think we're going to have to start over with a re-write of the rules from scratch."

"But you *will* win."

"I must."

"What about them?" She pointed at the sufferers below.

Azazel nodded agreement. "They are the reason why I must win."

"Baraqyel said they were the unhappy dead."

"They are. Heaven has coined a new word for them, in fact. They are the *damned*."

"How are they damned?"

Azazel sighed. "It means they have done terrible things in their earthly lives, and now that they are dead, they have to work it out."

"What does *work it out* mean?"

"I don't know." Azazel's eyes got a far-away look. "I haven't worked it out yet."

"Must they suffer?"

"They chose suffering themselves. What they need is someone to make their suffering worthwhile."

"Are you saying you're going to save them?"

Azazel stamped one hoof on the floor. "I definitely won't save them, nor will I save anyone else. I am not the saving kind. What I'm saying is that pain can be healing. Pain can unlock what is inside a person, it can release him of the burden of greater pain and set him in the path of recovery. Pain can, for instance, bring remorse. And I am very definitely the pain-inflicting kind."

A splash of water on the floor at her feet startled Qayna. She looked up to see tears glistening in the giant's eyes.

"I killed your son." She felt she had to say it.

"We killed him together. We both wanted to save him."

"Is that why you want to help …" Qayna gestured without looking at the twisting pile, "these people?"

"Someone must do this work," Azazel said. "I … it has been decreed that I shall be the one to do it."

"That sounds like a commission. Like a trust."

Azazel laughed a single short laugh, like a bark. "It is what it is."

"What happened to you?"

"I was tried. I was sentenced. I was condemned."

"You escaped."

"Here I am."

"Can *I* escape *my* punishment?"

Azazel sighed. "Ah, Qayna, I don't know. I think not. I think your life will last as long as this world's."

"And then?"

"And then a new heaven, and a new earth, and who knows what may be possible?"

Qayna felt tears in her own eyes now. "I think I'd better go," she said. "I don't think I'll come back this way again."

Azazel nodded slowly. "I will escort you out."

CHAPTER TEN

S top!" the Legate commanded.

From under his mantelletta, he produced a short stub of candle, burning red. Jane smelled cinnamon and blood, and froze in place where she stood.

"Adrian!" Jim shouted. He couldn't move, either.

"I'm working on it!" the wizard called back. He mumbled furiously under his breath, but without the ability to move his hands, write glyphs or do anything other than speak, Jane knew the organ player's arcane powers would be limited.

Only Jane's crow was unaffected. Bored, it flapped its wings and circled the rooftop among the various actors.

"Listen to me!" the Legate of Heaven hissed. "Stop struggling. We are on the same side!"

"Let me go, and we'll test that proposition." Jane struggled with the spell that bound the muscles of her body in place, but her ka was too weak to shatter the magic directly, and she couldn't reach anything in her saddlebags or her pockets.

"Piss off!" Jim phrased it more succinctly.

"I will leave you alone," the Legate said to the rock and roller. "I cannot promise what your father will say or do, but join me, and we will negotiate with him together."

Jim growled like a dog confronting a trespasser. "You think I'm an idiot, don't you?"

The Legate turned his face to Jane. "Give me the gun." His voice and face were soft. "You have walked a long and a hard road, Qayna, and I have the power to release you from it." His two golem sedan-slaves towered over him, and the Swordbearers towered over them all.

"I don't care to go to Hell," Jane said. "That seems like it would just be more of the same, with less variation in the scenery."

"Oblivion," the Legate promised. He nodded to his own frozen hand that held the sealed sheet of parchment. "You countersign the death letter, and you will cease to exist. Only give me the gun, so I can face the seraphim."

Jane's heart pounded in her ears so loud that she almost didn't hear the man's last words. This was a moment she had dreamed of for thousands of years, now, literally, within her grasp. She could lay down her heavy burden and just sink into nothingness. All she had to do was what the Legate asked. It wasn't even obedience to him, not really, it was just a trade like any other. She didn't think he could even use the gun anyway, though maybe … maybe he had some magic up his sleeve that would make him the Horn's wielder.

"Can I kill Raphael first?" she asked.

"Qayna, please," the angel protested. He couldn't move, either. None of them could, below the neck, until the candle burned out.

The Legate looked closely into her eyes. "Do you really want to?"

"Yes," she said. "Yes, I do. But I'd prefer he get the Hell treatment, rather than oblivion."

"I can't do it." The Legate shook his head. "But I can promise you that in one minute, if you give me the gun, you won't care anymore. You won't care, you won't worry, you won't remember. You won't anything. You will simply vanish."

Jane wanted it. She wanted it really, really bad.

But in her heart of hearts, she knew she couldn't take the offer. Instead, she cursed.

Her Adamic swear-word snuffed out the candle, and she shot her hand for the Calamity Horn.

Raphael went for his gun.

The golems rushed forward.

Jane grabbed the Calamity Horn, knowing that she had only moments before the Legate re-lit his candle and also certain that the Messenger would clear leather first. That was fine with her. She never dished out what she couldn't take.

Bang! Bang!

The angel in the Deputy's body got off two shots and Jane felt them both hit, two mule-kicks to the chest. Then she had the Model 1910 in her hands and began firing, only not at Raphael—she shot at the Swordbearers.

She threw the first bullet over Raphael's shoulder, right at the chest of the Bearer behind him. More of Raphael's shots struck her as she fell spinning, shooting arm extended and throwing out thirty-two caliber rounds like a centrifuge of madness and spiritual plague.

Jim shrieked and staggered away, wrestling with the sounds in his head, and gunfire exploded from where the rest of the rock and roll band stood. Twitch burst into falcon form and sprang away from the meat packing plant.

The Bearers of the Sword were gigantic, imposing, more like towers than like men. That made them virtually impossible to miss. Jane focused on each shot as she took it and not on the damage the preceding shots had done, but she couldn't miss, out of the corner of her eye, the bright red streaks that appeared in the flaming white persons of the Swordbearers. Nor could she miss the shattering shrieks of indignant pain.

The Bearers of the Sword weren't used to being hurt.

For Ainok's sake, she enjoyed their surprise and indignation.

As Jane fired the seventh and final shot, she crashed to the gravel. Another of Raphael's bullets hit her in the shoulder and she grunted in pain, and then a bright red spark kicked the Legate's candle again into flame.

Flat on her back, Jane froze again. A few feet to one side, she heard Jim screaming. The Legate's kilt-clad golems hulked over her, eyes dull and fists clenched and raised to punch her.

"Foolish!" the Legate snapped at her. "Do you know what you risk?"

Jane coughed blood into her mouth and spat it at him.

Then the first of the Bearers' swords crashed down into the rooftop of the building. Chunks of concrete and steel, and bushels of wet gravel, exploded in all directions. In the violence of the suddenly-thrashing air, the candle snuffed out once more.

"Stop!" the Legate shouted.

Jane whipped a knife straight up into one golem's face, rolling to the side as she did. It collapsed backward with a wet murmur, and she came up with a second blade in her hand, which she snapped into his companion's face. She holstered the Calamity Horn and stepped past the magical creatures. She moved briskly; she'd taken them by surprise, but not seriously injured the golems.

A circle of flaming white and red closed in on Fine Cuts, Inc. The Swordbearers' faces were hidden behind their blank helmets, but they expressed their surprise and anger—or perhaps their mechanical, reflexive self-defense instincts—admirably with their upraised weapons.

Jim struggled to his feet, gripping his head between his hands. He hadn't lost his grip on the hoof, which was good. Raphael ejected a spent clip from his gun and fumbled to slot in a full replacement.

"Stop!" the Legate cried again. He incanted something, raising his hands against the advancing Swordbearers. In one hand he held the candle; in the other was Jane's death letter.

Roaring, Jane charged.

She almost tripped over her own saddlebags, but grabbed them on the run. Raphael fired at her again—idiot, he was wasting ammunition—and Twitch, now in her horse form, had clamped her big horsey teeth into Jim's shirt and was dragging him away.

Another flaming sword plunged into the rooftop, this one spiking down like a hammered nail. It missed Jane by several feet and the shockwaves made her stumble. She dropped her shoulder and rammed it into the Legate's belly.

"Oomph!" he barked.

She wrapped her arms around him and kept going.

The rooftop beneath Jane's feet buckled and twisted; she ran faster, gaining strength as she went. Fire at her heels scorched her, and she had no more attention to pay to what the rock and rollers were up to.

She only hoped she had enough fire within her, in her ka, to get where she wanted to go.

The Legate pounded on Jane's back with balled fists. She ignored him, except to squeeze as hard as she could, until she felt soft snaps that might have been ribs giving way. If the man had no breath, he wouldn't be casting any spells on her.

She incanted, murmuring words in Adamic as she reached the lip of the roof. Below her stretched the pocked and pitted asphalt, the water in the craters trembling with the shocks of the violence being inflicted on the building, but reflecting wavering images of the burning columns that were the Swordbearers.

Perfectly serviceable mirrors.

More bullets chomped into Jane's back as she jumped from the building—

arced through the air head-first, squeezing the Legate tight as any girl ever squeezed her teddy bear, saddlebags flopping awkwardly around them—

struck a puddle the size of a small garden pond—

and fell through, slamming to the ground on the hard stone floor of the Outer Bounds of the Mirror Queendom.

"Uuuununnnnhnhhh," the Legate wheezed in breathless pain.

Jane rolled away from him in the patchy gray light, aching all over from the exertion and from the gunshot wounds. She wondered how many times Raphael had been able to hit her; she owed him that much more revenge, the next time she caught him.

She ejected her clip and groped in a pocket of her duster for bullets.

"You broke all my ribs," the Legate whined.

Jane ignored him.

"Welcome," she heard a cold voice say.

Jane looked up. "Not again." Her words were wet, incomprehensible through the blood bubbling from her lips.

A woman stood before her, tall and slender and fair. Hair like peacock feathers swept back in an iridescent halo from her high forehead. She didn't appear to be dressed so much as to have leaves plastered to her body, all over, and in her right hand she leaned on something that shimmered and was slippery to look at, but might have been a spear or a bolt of lightning.

Between Jane and the woman, and encircling Jane and the Legate, was a ring of fey fighters, leather-clad spear-warriors with animal tails. They all snarled at Jane, and she ignored them, slowly thumbing bullets into her clip.

"You're Mab," she said, when her lungs had cleared of blood enough to talk.

"You are the Marked Woman."

"I'd prefer you let me pass in peace."

"I'd prefer that you not shoot me."

"Fair enough." Jane snapped the clip back into the gun, reholstered it, and stood. She was shaky on her feet, but stayed upright. She found a handkerchief in one pocket and spat blood into it, to avoid spitting on the floor.

No point being gratuitously disrespectful; surely, enough opportunity for genuine disrespect would arrive unaided.

"Idiot," the Legate cursed her. He lay crumpled on the floor, breathing fast and shallow and holding an arm that looked shattered.

Beside him lay the letter. Jane stooped, picked it up, and popped the seal with her finger.

Inside, the parchment was blank.

"Liar," she said, and dropped the parchment on him.

"My cause is just!" he insisted. Shuffling and wheezing, he managed to tumble to his knees. "It's the greatest cause of all."

"You want to be God."

"No, that isn't it!" The Legate's eyes blazed bright. "I want there to *be* a God! I want a Heaven that is compassionate, a God who cares, a throne room that isn't empty!"

"Like I said," Jane muttered.

"Have you no feelings?"

"No," Jane lied. "I did once, and you people stomped them into nothing."

"I can get you a death letter," the Legate promised. "Yes, this one was a fake, but I can get you a real one. I need your help. *We* need your help. The whole *world* needs you. Won't you show mercy? Would you rather that the seraphim run Heaven than me?"

"I would rather," Jane said heavily, "that you stop. If you need a cause, sell cookies for the Girl Scouts."

"You insult me!" The Legate rose, limping, to his feet.

"Take him away." Mab gestured with her glittering spear and her soldiers closed in around the Legate.

The Legate's face turned purple with rage as fairy weapons prodded him and fairy hands grabbed. "You insult *Heaven!*" he spluttered.

"That's rich," Jane grunted, and then the Queen's Rangers whisked the Legate away. The echoes and faraway sounds of the arrest continued for some time.

The two women were left with a much smaller retinue of Rangers.

Mab examined Jane closely. "There is fairy blood on your hands," she pronounced.

Jane sighed. "Okay," she admitted.

"I am not familiar with the *okay* defense." Mab frowned. "Do you mean that you rejoice in the death of my Rangers?"

Jane chuckled.

"I am not amused. Do you find it acceptable to kill my people?"

"I rejoice in no death, Your Majesty," Jane said. "Sometimes I get a little tickled by the prospect of my own."

Mab considered this. "I understand."

"Are you going to get in my way?"

"Are you going to attack my people?"

Jane sighed. "I just want out. That's all I've ever wanted."

"Ever?"

"Well, for six thousand years."

Mab shared an expression with Jane that was close to a smile. "I understand."

Jane reached for her quicksilver.

"I was going to make you an offer," Mab said. "I was going to bring you to your horse in exchange for the hoof of Azazel."

Jane arched an eyebrow. "I don't have the hoof of Azazel."

"That's why I can't make you the offer," Mab agreed.

"What do you want the hoof for?" Jane asked. "I thought you people were friends of Hell? Or are you just doing the Morning Star's bidding now?"

"That is not your affair." Mab stared coldly down her slender nose at Jane.

Jane shrugged. Her bleeding had stopped. The crow perched on a stone lintel over her head and stared down at her cruelly.

She felt like she was taking bait, but she had to ask. "Does that mean my horse is alive?"

Mab grinned. "What would it be worth to be led to her?"

Jane tapped the bead of quicksilver into her palm, feeling a small grim note of satisfaction that Mab pulled back slightly at the sight of it. "Nothing," she bluffed. "I'll find her on my own."

Mab laughed a silvery string of bell-like notes. "Very good, Marked Woman." The Queen of the Shadowless Palace beckoned forward one of her Rangers, a chestnut-haired youth with a bushy squirrel's tail. "Take her to the Thracian Mare."

Jane inclined her head politely and then poured the bead back into its vial. "Your Majesty."

"Ride well."

"Enjoy your conversation with the Legate."

Jane followed Squirrel through the Outer Bounds. She wouldn't have admitted it to Mab, but she was grateful for the guide—without it, she'd have spent hours, no doubt, waiting for her ka to recuperate so she could find her way, and then waited hours more at the gate to be able to pass through. In that time, who knows who or what might have come through into the Outer Bounds chasing her? Instead, she slugged calmly through the maze of stairwells, bridges, corridors and chambers with her saddlebags slung over her shoulder, letting her ka heal along with her indomitable body, while Squirrel *chucked* his teeth together and looked at her repeatedly over his slender shoulder.

Through the mirror-gate to which the fairy led her, Jane peered and saw that the Bearers of the Sword had gone. That was enough for her—she nodded to Squirrel, incanted her transition spell and slipped back into the sorghum fields outside Dodge City, Kansas.

She stepped from the rear view mirror of the destroyed deputies' car. The mirror was no longer attached to the body of the vehicle, but lay on the side of the road alone. For that matter, there was no longer a body of the car—just smaller and larger fragments of wreckage.

The same was true of Fine Cuts, Inc., Jane saw as she walked towards it. The enormous swords of Heaven's enforcers had smashed it to rubble and left it burning. Fire was beginning to spread to the adjacent fields, too, and in the distance, Jane heard the wailing sirens of emergency response vehicles.

Jane stopped at the edge of the pocked parking lot and whistled.

After two seconds' delay, the Mare cantered around the back of the plant, baring its predators' teeth at her and whinnying in something that almost sounded like pleasure.

Jane whinnied back and patted the dangerous, violent animal on its face. The horse's flanks were bloody, so Jane left the saddlebags on her own shoulder, took the Mare by the reins and started to lead it down the highway.

"Good girl," she said.

With a guttural coughing, the Dodge van rattled out from the other side of the plant, shocks taking a beating as the driver gunned it over the craters. At the edge of the highway, Jane and the van met, and the rock and rollers braked.

Jane was careful not to be too obvious about it, but she let her gun hand drift down and idle not far from the butt of the pistol.

Jim slid the van door open from the inside. Within, Jane saw Mike and Eddie in front and the wizard, Adrian, in back, squinting at her suspiciously through his sorcerous monocle. Twitch must be flying around under her own power, Jane guessed.

Jim scooted back and made room on the middle seat beside him. He gestured at it invitingly and arched an eyebrow. He looked a bit like his father, Azazel, she thought. But he looked a lot like Jacob. He looked just like Jacob might have looked, if Jacob had ever had the chance to grow up.

Eddie cranked down the window. The guitar player smiled, but in an *I-don't-trust-you-much* sort of way, and he kept his hands out of sight. Jane remembered his pistol and paid attention.

"Thanks," she said. "I'd be more trouble than I'm worth."

"I doubt that," Eddie said, in a voice that sounded like he believed her totally. "You want a lift? We might owe you."

Jane shook her head. "I ride alone. Hadn't you heard?"

Eddie nodded. "Still, Jim has this thing for taking in strays. He likes people with problems. Especially the damnation sort of problem."

Jane frowned. She could hear the sirens closer now. "I don't know whether I'm damned or not. We didn't have damnation when

I was a kid, so I don't know where I stand. My big problem isn't that at all—"

"Your big problem is you can't die," Eddie cut her off.

"*Chingado.*"

"Bullseye," she said.

Eddie nodded. "Take care of yourself." He ground his window back up again, Jim nodded, and then they were in motion, rolling onto the highway and away.

Above the taillights of the Dodge, she could make out two birds flying away. One was Twitch, a white-winged raptor with a silver horse's tail; the other was a large black crow.

"Come on, girl." Jane turned and led her mount into the sorghum fields. She didn't have the strength of ka to put together any useful wards, and she could see the lights of the police cars and fire trucks now. She'd feel better after a couple of hours of light walking, and then she'd put together appropriate spells for traveling.

The Thracian Mare neighed a slight protest.

"Don't worry, he'll be back," Jane acknowledged. "The crow will always be back."

ABOUT THE AUTHOR

D.J. Butler (Dave) is a novelist living in the Rocky Mountain northwest. His training is in law, and he worked as a securities lawyer at a major international firm and inhouse at two multinational semiconductor manufacturers before taking up writing fiction. He is a lover of language and languages, a guitarist and self-recorder, and a serious reader. He is married to a powerful and clever woman and together they have three devious children.

Dave writes fantasy, science fiction, space opera, steampunk, cyberpunk, superhero, alternate history, dystopian fiction, horror and related genres for all audiences. His novels *Crecheling* and *City of the Saints* are available from WordFire Press, and his middle reader steampunk adventure series, The Extraordinary Journeys of Clockwork Charlie, launches soon with the novel *The Kidnap Plot* (Knopf, 2016).

Read about all of Dave's fiction projects at:

http://davidjohnbutler.com.

OTHER WORDFIRE PRESS TITLES BY D.J. BUTLER

Rock Band Fights Evil:
Hellhound On My Tail
Snake Handlin' Man
Devil Sent the Rain

Crecheling

Our list of other WordFire Press authors and titles is always growing.
To find out more and to see our selection of titles, visit us at:

wordfirepress.com

OTHER WORDFIRE PRESS TITLES BY D.J. BUTLER

Rock Band Fights Evil:

Hellhound On My Tail

Snake Handlin' Man

Devil Sent the Rain

Crecheling

Our list of other WordFire Press authors and titles is always growing. To find out more and to see our selection of titles, visit us at:

wordfirepress.com

www.ingramcontent.com/pod-product-compliance
Lightning Source LLC
Chambersburg PA
CBHW020532120726
47904CB00003B/1039